SOUND
FRIENDSHIPS

SOUND FRIENDSHIPS

The Story of Willa and Her Hearing Dog

Elizabeth Yates

Edited by Gloria Repp
Bob Jones University Press, Greenville, South Carolina 29614

Sound Friendships:
The Story of Willa and Her Hearing Dog

Special thanks to Brian Cleveland of Dog Trainers Workshop
and to his dog Ryan, who posed for the cover.

Photographs by Koko Productions, Judy Savage
Cover by John Roberts
Project editor: Christine Leaman

CURR
HV
2509
.Y37
1992

ISBN 0-89084-650-2

20   19   18   17   16   15   14   13   12   11   10   9   8   7

Books for Young People by Elizabeth Yates

Amos Fortune, Free Man
Someday You'll Write
Sam's Secret Journal
Prudence Crandall
Sarah Whitcher's Story
We, the People
Carolina's Courage
The Journeyman
Hue & Cry
Sound Friendships

Foreword

What is a Hearing Dog? Fifty years ago the question might well have been asked, "What is a Seeing Eye Dog?" Today, bred and trained to guide blind persons, Seeing Eye Dogs are seen on city streets and college campuses, in stores, offices, planes, and buses. Familiar and respected for what they are and do, they give independence and mobility to individuals for whom loss of sight has meant severe limitations. Now Hearing Dogs are becoming better known as well, giving independence and security to people who are deaf in a manner that compensates in some measure for their deprivation.

The first known Hearing Dog was a German shepherd from Stormcroft Kennels named Skippy. Skippy was owned by the Prichard family of Colorado and was trained by Sally Terroux in 1968 to help their deaf daughter.

Despite this initial activity in the late sixties, the training of Hearing Dogs was neglected until 1974 when Agnes McGrath, a Master Trainer, was asked by the Minnesota Society for the Prevention of Cruelty to Animals to do a feasibility study to determine whether dogs could be trained to aid deaf people. She proved that they could, using six carefully trained dogs. After she demonstrated what these dogs could do for people who are deaf, the first training center was established under the auspices of the American Humane Society in Denver, Colorado. In time, other states started similar centers, and today there are about thirty functioning programs across the United States.

The American Humane Society no longer operates a training center, but in conjunction with the Delta Society and Pedigree Dog Foods, it has established the Hearing Dog Resource Center and Advisory Board. This organization serves as an information and advocacy center offering a nationwide referral service. Recent meetings of the Hearing Dog Advisory Board have brought Hearing-Dog program specialists, recipients, and advocates together to discuss national guidelines, identification for the dogs, and training procedures.

When Agnes McGrath trained the first six dogs, it was her hope that a time would come when Hearing Dogs for people who are deaf would be as fully recognized as dog guides for people who are blind. Her hope has been partially realized: assurance came when the Colorado legislature passed a law that dogs trained and certified as Hearing Dogs be accepted in all public places and conveyances.

One state after another has enacted similar laws. The federal government gave its recognition when the Internal Revenue Service ruled that expenses incurred for such dogs are tax deductible and when the American Disabilities Act was passed in May of 1990.

During their first decade and a half of service, Hearing Dogs have proved their worth by assisting some thirty-five hundred hearing-impaired people. Alerting their masters to sound in their environment, as well as becoming the visual sign of their deafness, these dogs have become a valued tool to educate the public about this invisible handicap that affects more than 26 million Americans.

The concept of Hearing Dogs and the credibility of their use as a support system for people who are hearing impaired have become more widely known and accepted during the past five-year period. This awareness is the result of intense efforts by the New England Assistance Dog Service program (and all Hearing Dog organizations) to educate the public. These efforts have included articles in national publications, television exposure, demonstrations to civic groups, and, most importantly, the example of our graduates themselves, who use their Hearing Dogs for independence and security in their daily lives.

* * * * *

It is our pleasure to introduce this perceptive and inspiring book by Elizabeth Yates, whose insights reveal the bonds that can grow so quickly between a Hearing Dog and its owner. The people and dogs in this story might have been those at any one of the centers functioning across the United States. Although there are minor differences in procedure, the common elements of staff commitment and dedication pervade them all.

When a deaf person and a Hearing Dog are matched, they become a team, and this deeply personal happening is a scenario that is duplicated at each center. The shared qualities of special communication, mutual love, and loyalty are demonstrated by these teams regardless of where or how they have been trained.

Elizabeth Yates made frequent visits to the center at West Boylston, Massachusetts, to observe first the training of the dogs and then their matching. Conversations with new owners and interviews with people who had owned dogs for several years gave her much of the material with which she has told her story. With rare understanding of the mind of the dog and sensitive insight into the problems of deafness, she has captured the essence of this remarkable coming together of need and service. Into the warp of facts she has woven the woof of a story that has touched us all.

Since 1990 our work has been widened to meet the needs of many other people who are physically disabled. New dogs called Service Dogs are being trained to help people who use wheelchairs, canes, and crutches. Just as Dog Guides and Hearing Dogs become the ''eyes'' and ''ears'' for their masters, Service Dogs become the ''arms'' and ''legs'' for their masters. They pick up dropped articles, turn light switches on and off, carry items, and pull wheelchairs. In order to reflect this new service, our name has been changed to the New England Assistance Dog Service, or NEADS, and we continue to place these very special dogs with very special people.

SHEILA O'BRIEN,
Executive Director,
NEADS

For more information please contact:

N E A D S

P.O. Box 213
West Boylston, MA 01583
(508) 835-3304 Voice or TDD

Chapter One

It happened in a moment of time, and because of it, all the moments of her life were different. A firecracker tied to Willa's pigtail made a shattering sound, the last sound she was ever to hear. She was only fourteen at the time; now ten years had passed, and she had grown accustomed to her limitations.

Willa could still remember and hold in her mind much that had been the music of life—the wind in the trees, the laughter of children, her name being called. And there were other memories, things she did not want to remember—the many operations, her head swathed in bandages, the visits to specialists, and the anxious faces of her parents. She realized dimly that during her growing-up years they had overprotected her, as in their anguish they had tried to make up for what she had lost.

Although the otic nerve in her ear had been destroyed by the explosion, she learned to communicate with others by means of speech reading and sign language; and a small device implanted in her ear enabled her to keep her own voice modulated. These skills and others helped her through high school, then into business school, where a practical course assured her of work as a secretary.

After her father had died and then her mother, the family home seemed too big for Willa, too much to keep up; so she moved to a ground-floor apartment. It had a small back yard that would be nice for Poppy, who was getting to be an old dog, and she would have a place to grow some flowers. At twenty-five, alone and in new surroundings, Willa faced the self she would live with for the rest of her life.

"You'll make out all right," people had said in their well-meaning way, writing it in letters, since they were more sure of the written word getting through to her. "You have, all along. Living by yourself is just one more thing to get used to. Let us know when we can help. Give yourself time."

Oh, they were all so kind, but did they know, could they ever really know, what it was like to live walled into a world without so much as a whisper to penetrate its silence?

When Willa talked to Poppy, the old dog seemed to understand, but when she conversed with people, they often became irritated, raising their voices as if that would help. Willa knew that she was slow at speech reading and that when she did not answer right away people were annoyed. Since she could talk, neighbors forgot that she could not hear, and often they called to her on the street. But she didn't know someone was there unless he waved or gave a visible signal. Acquaintances began to fall away, and a friend explained, ''They think you're snobbish. They just don't understand.''

Willa withdrew more and more into herself, building up a wall of suspicion. And because people did not talk to her, she thought they were talking about her. Gradually her links with those around her fell away; she began to read more, she became interested in cooking, and she planted flowers that gave off fragrance. She could see, she told herself; she could taste and smell, and she could touch Poppy and feel a response. Sometimes it seemed that they did not look at each other so much as into each other, sharing their peculiar quiet.

Television meant little to Willa except that it gave her practice in speech reading; but there were some programs, generally foreign ones, that had captions below the pictures. One evening while she watched the news, Willa's attention was arrested by a scene of dogs working with people in a large open field. She eyed them curiously. They were not show dogs but seemed to be an odd mixture of breeds ranging from large to small. They were not Seeing Eye Dogs either, for they were on long leashes instead of harnesses.

There was something about the people, too, that attracted her. She knew how a person with impaired hearing tended to walk, cautiously, turning the head frequently from right to left, often using the shadow cast by an approaching pedestrian to edge more to one side. But these people were walking with more confident strides. As she watched them, each one leading a dog on an orange leash, a caption flashed across the screen and she read it eagerly.

She learned from the caption that these dogs had been trained to function as ears for their owners who were deaf. Now Willa watched more intently. When the hour ended, the name and address of the New England Assistance Dog Service program was given, and interested viewers were urged to write for information. Willa sat down and wrote the letter; then she decided to mail it right away. Although she rarely went out after dark because it was so hard to watch for traffic, tonight an unfamiliar surge of hope overcame the fear that had been her safeguard. And her heart heard the thud made by the letter as it dropped into the box.

An answer came soon, and its warmth assured Willa that there were people ready to help provide a way out of her prison. She learned that she might indeed qualify for a dog, and that at her request the NEADS organization would send her an application form.

The first exchange of letters was followed by others, filled with questions. She could understand that they would want to know her age, health, and occupation, but why was it so important for them to know how she felt about animals? She had grown up with the family dog, she told them. She found it comforting to write about Poppy, knowing they would understand what the old dog had meant to her for many years.

Poppy had always been there, fed by anyone who happened to be in the kitchen near feeding time, responding to anyone who called if she had a mind to, enjoying being petted. As for making much of her, it was no more than making much of a piece of furniture. Yet, after the explosion, Willa remembered that something had begun to deepen between herself and Poppy. It was as if they needed each other, the one who did not speak, the other who did not hear. Not long ago when Poppy had died, Willa cried as she had never cried for herself.

As she finished her letter about Poppy, she smiled. Now she would have another dog in her life: a dog trained to meet her needs, a dog with whom she would have to train.

Soon an outreach worker from the regional NEADS office came to call on Willa. They communicated easily with each other through speech reading and signing.

The worker explained why she had come. "We have a group of dogs that we've been working with for five months, and we know a good deal about them, their personalities, and their temperaments," she said to Willa. "They are as different as people are. Now we need to know about you so we can match a dog to you, for our satisfaction is in the perfect match."

Then the worker described the dogs and the screening they had gone through before they were accepted for training. After being trained they would be certified as Hearing Dogs. "Now, by law, these dogs are permitted to accompany their deaf owners to any place, in any conveyance, in all fifty states," she explained. "They are identified by their orange collars, leashes, and capes with the words in big black letters: HEARING DOG. The owner carries an ID card as well."

"Those were the dogs I saw on TV, weren't they?" Willa asked.

"Some of them, yes."

Eagerly Willa questioned the worker about the dogs.

"They are strays for the most part, obtained from animal shelters," she answered. "Many of them have had lives of neglect and abandonment. Because of their need for love, they seem to have a special capacity to respond to love. Sometimes we get a dog from someone who is going away and must find it a home, or from a breeder who has a misfit." She smiled. "They are a motley bunch, and you can't always identify the breeds. In a dog's tail or its color you may see traces of a spaniel or a collie, a lab or a hound or a poodle, but often there is no clue at all."

Willa mentioned the pint-sized poodle she had noticed on the television show.

"That's Molly, a peekapoo, white as a snowdrift and weighing all of ten pounds," the worker said. "We found her walking down a city street, obviously abandoned. No matter how hard we searched, we never did discover her owner, but she responded to training. She's been our demonstration dog for six years. 'Molly gives lectures' they say at the office, since she goes along with us to clubs and organizations to show what a Hearing Dog can do and to enlist support." She gave Willa a searching look. "Molly would never do for you."

"No, I'd like a knee-high dog whose head my hand could rest on."

She nodded. "A gentle dog with outgoing ways. A dog with a sense of humor, perhaps?"

Willa smiled suddenly. "You seem to know my needs."

"Let me tell you the procedure," the worker said. "When a stray is found, it is taken to the animal shelter and fed and washed while we try to discover its owner. When we are ready to train a new group of dogs, we visit the shelter to screen the ones recently found; we want to determine their potential as working animals. For our purposes they should be young, from eight months to two years old, and range in size from small, like Molly, to about fifty-five pounds."

Fifty-five pounds, Willa thought. Perhaps that is what my dog will weigh.

"They're all appealing," she went on. "Most of them have already been house-trained and have some experience of life. We can soon tell which ones may be suitable for the program; and they are taken to a veterinarian, who keeps them in quarantine for two weeks and verifies their ages by the soundness of their teeth. Then they're spayed or neutered, given a thorough health examination to be sure there is no latent disease or problem, x-rayed, and given all their necessary shots. When the vet pronounces them ready, we bring the dogs to our kennels to start them on a training period that will last for five months. During this time of working and testing, the trainers discover a great deal about each dog's personality and temperament."

Willa wanted to know more. It was hard for her to believe that there could be such differences in dogs. "What are they tested for?" she asked.

"Willingness to work: fetching an article, for instance, and doing it not for fun or on impulse but at the trainer's command. Curiosity: that's almost the same as intelligence.

Ability to localize sounds: any dog will be alert to a sound, but finding where it comes from is something else.'' The worker glanced at the mirror on Willa's door. ''We also show the dog an image in a mirror—that tells us something. Then we might play a few notes on a harmonica or run a clockwork toy across the floor and see how the dog reacts. Or, while petting the dog, we might pull a hair gently. Does he snap or bare his teeth? Or does he just turn his head toward the one who is stroking him? The tests show us whether a dog wants to please, and this is essential; energy, self-confidence, and stability are all essentials too. And always, underlying everything else, we are asking ourselves: Is this a dog that can accept responsibility? The tests are hard and constant through the time of training, and only one dog out of four passes.''

''Only one out of four?'' asked Willa in surprise. ''Why?''

''Well, a dog may be good at sounds one day, but the next day it couldn't care less; it has to be good every day. Don't worry,'' she added, ''the trainers learn to love the dogs as they work with them. So, if some fail the program, everything is done to find homes for them where companionship is more important than responsibility.''

''This whole program must require a lot of love,'' Willa said.

''Yes, and money. It takes months to care for and board the dogs, first at the vet's, then in our kennels during the training. With our program the cost is $4,000 for each dog. Not very many applicants are able to pay that much, so we really need sponsors. Clubs, organizations, businesses, and sometimes individuals help us out. Every student coming to the program is asked to pay at least $150 for his or her dog.'' She paused. ''Does all this alarm you?''

''Not yet,'' Willa said, ''but I was wondering if I would pass your test to be deserving of such a dog.''

The worker smiled. ''You have already, in your obvious need and in what you have told us about Poppy. And you already have a sponsor too. When you gave us your place of business as a reference, we wrote them about the program and your interest in it. They agreed to be your sponsor.''

''Oh!'' Willa exclaimed. ''How good of them! And the dog? What kind of dog will you choose for me?''

''I have a picture to show you. We think you and Honey will be a good match.'' The worker handed Willa a snapshot.

''A golden retriever,'' she breathed, scarcely able to utter the words.

''Not quite. Honey's grandparents and her mother were probably purebreds but her father wasn't.''

''It doesn't matter.''

''Of course not! When you meet her, you'll see the best of the known and unknown strains in her.''

''Oh yes! When?''

The worker gave Willa the date for the next class and information about where it would be held. ''You have plenty of time to make your arrangements,'' she concluded.

Time! thought Willa. Now it was not something to be endured or lived through, but something in which every moment would count.

The next day at work, Willa asked for and received a month's leave of absence. Then she made her preparations. She wrote letters to friends, explaining where she would be and what she would be doing "for my vacation." She paid a visit to the bank, returned books to the library, and made a few purchases—one of them an alarm clock—and packed two suitcases. Of the two, the larger one was lighter. It contained the blanket she had brought to be Honey's bed, a six-foot webbed leash, and the alarm clock she had been told to bring.

Now she was ready to leave for the bus station. When she closed the door of her apartment behind her, it was with a sense of subdued excitement, knowing that the next time she opened that door she would not be alone. A companion would be with her, a companion who was going to be part of her life.

Chapter Two

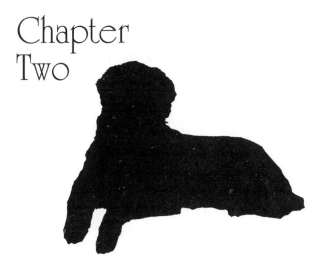

There were six in the class at the training center, and they met that first afternoon knowing nothing about each other. But one thing in common united them before they knew each other's names.

Four students had degrees of impairment that required them to wear hearing aids; one besides Willa was profoundly deaf. All could speech read to an extent, and some could sign. Willa was the only person from New England; others had come from much farther away. They met with smiles and shaking of hands, the universal language.

"When will I get my dog?" was the question each person asked the instructor. They had all seen pictures and been given descriptions of their dogs, and each person carried the required six-foot leash ready to be attached to a collar.

"Tomorrow," said the instructor with a smile. "We have a lot to do today."

Each student had been given a folder with papers to be studied; some were to be signed. The most important and immediate paper was the contract that described their agreement with the Hearing Dog program.

CONTRACT. I, the undersigned, hereby agree to take full responsibility for the continuous care and training of the Hearing Dog I obtained from the New England Assistance Dog Service. I understand that the program can decertify the dog with no reimbursement to me or my contributing sponsors in the event that the dog is abused or neglected or not being used for the purpose for which it was trained.

Signature_____ Date_____

The instructor handed out other papers, too full of questions for Willa to answer right away, but the instructor said that the forms could be filled out during free time in the evenings. Willa felt as if she had gone back to school—which, in a way, she had.

Then the instructor showed a sequence of slides. They told the story of a woman coming to the program to get a dog, and the words of the sound track were supplemented by the instructor's signing. The students were asked to imagine themselves in the place of the woman on the screen, because they would soon be doing what she did.

"When you meet your dog tomorrow, don't be surprised if you are ignored," the instructor told them. "There is a whole new relationship to be established. The dog might be thinking, 'You're not my trainer—what have I got to do with you?' That is where your long leash comes into use. Snap it onto the dog's chain-link collar and tie the other end to your belt. Then it will be like an umbilical cord. For the first few days your dog will be with you at all times. Only when you go to bed or take a shower will you release the connections. This is *bonding*. During this time the dog becomes an extension of you. You will feed the dog at the same time every day in your own room, you will walk with your dog, and you will discipline your dog. That first distrustful look the dog gives you will change before long to one of complete trust.''

The instructor smiled reassuringly. ''This may not happen with you tomorrow, but you can see it happening with the woman on the screen and it will be the same for you. Relationships deepen through days of training, and when it is time for you to leave, you and your dog will know that you have become a team.''

An early supper followed, and then the students were dismissed for the night. Each one had work to do, and for all of them morning could not come soon enough, the morning when they would be matched with their dogs.

Willa sat at her desk, reading and answering the questions on the sheets given her. Some of the questions seemed elementary, but there were others that made her search for the right answer and then admit that she really would not know until the instructor had taken the students further through the course. As she thought about Honey and the routine that would be hers as a working dog, she remembered Poppy and the casual life she had led. When someone opened the door, Poppy went out and stayed as long as she liked. She returned when she pleased, and no one knew or cared where she went or what she did, except for the last year when her range had been the garden. Honey's life would have a definite pattern, and it would be up to Willa to maintain it.

Willa put the papers back into their folder and got ready for bed. That afternoon in class the instructor had recommended a book on dog training; she would read it for a while. She read until sleep began to overtake her; then she put out the light and reached down to smooth her hand over the blanket on the floor by her bed. "Good night, Honey," she whispered. It was easy to pretend for one more night. Tomorrow Honey would be there.

* * * * *

It was only a short distance across an open field to the kennels. Once there, the students were told to wait outside, and their dogs would be brought to them.

One after another the dogs came—Laddie, an almost collie; Cookie, a small dog that looked like a cross between a beagle and a spaniel; Emily, a labrador with a trace of husky; Ebony, black, smooth-haired, stately, and quite unidentifiable; Jack, a white shepherd with drooping ears; and Honey. Trainers led them to their new owners and showed how the link collar should be put on and the long leash attached. The dogs were more interested in their trainers than in the people to whom they were led, but after the leashes were attached and the trainers withdrew, they seemed to realize that a new thing was happening. Some dogs barked for attention, others jumped against the strange legs, and some circled around in a whirl of uncertainty.

Sound Friendships

For Willa, time—both her enemy and her ally—stood still. She was aware of a tug at her heart like the tug Honey was making on the leash; then she reached down and drew in the leash. She laid her hand on the golden head. Surprised, Honey looked up at her. A warm soft tongue caressed the new hand, and in that moment a transfer of affection was made. Willa looked away quickly. Had she been alone she would have let the tears flow, but now there was too much to attend to and the instructor was speaking.

"Call your dogs by their names," he said. "Go off with them across the field for a few minutes. Let them get to know who you are."

One of the dogs walked sedately. Two ran in circles, tangling leashes and legs, another sat down in puzzlement; the shepherd pulled hard, wanting to run. Honey leaned against Willa, raised her head again, and their eyes met and held.

A trainer approached them. "You don't need to go across the field if you don't want to. You've made eye contact, and that is the most important of all." He smiled. "There's no question in Honey's mind that she belongs to you and you belong to her."

When the others returned, the first lesson was given. "Tie your leashes to your belts and we'll begin work," said the instructor. Everyone walked back to the house. After they sat down in the big room, the dogs were put in a down-stay position and the students listened to the instructor. There were no slides this time, just words spoken clearly, with signing to supplement the words.

15

"Your dogs have had three months of obedience training, and they know the basic commands: *heel, sit, down,
stay, come,*" explained the instructor. "Their vocabularies
will increase with specific needs as you work with them.
Tell is a fairly new word, so is *fetch,* and you will use them
both in time. *No* means business, and it will be most effec-
tive when you combine it with your facial expression of
displeasure and the shakedown."

"What's that?" someone asked.

"It's what a mother dog does with her puppies when
she wants to teach them a lesson they'll not forget." The
instructor took the dog nearest her, put both hands on the
scruff of the dog's neck, looked intently into the eyes gazing
at her, and shook the dog, not roughly or hurtfully, but so
the meaning was manifest. "Gently does it, every time."

The instructor's glance went around the group to be
sure she had their attention. "Another command will be
given, not by you but by the situation, and that is *think.*
When you're walking with your dog on the street, you may
be surprised that instead of heeling as it has been doing,
your dog sits down and refuses to move. What sound has
come to those attentive ears, what warning? When you turn
and see a car approaching from behind, you will know that
danger has been averted."

Willa remembered how hesitant she'd been to go out at
night, and her hand tightened on Honey's leash. "Don't
question your dog," continued the instructor. "Act. You
have been giving commands that have been faithfully followed, but there will be times when your dog may give you
a command. Reward with praise and a great show of affection. Your dogs want to please you, but let me warn you

that they are smart—if they weren't they wouldn't have been chosen for the program—and they'll test you sometimes in ways of their own devising.''

That afternoon everyone went back to the field to practice the commands and learn the hand signals that went with them. The commands had to be repeated over and over again, but through the repetition the dogs learned the tone of new voices, the feel of new hands. Some dogs might still look longingly at their trainers who stood at a distance, but gradually all of them gave full attention to the person they walked beside. Later on in the big room, the dogs settled down comfortably by their owners, finding that six feet of leash was sufficient freedom. Some licked their paws and other parts of their bodies; most of them flattened out in sleep.

''At all times,'' the instructor began, ''your dog must know that you are the boss. Reward good behavior with little treats and praise, then with praise only. Accept the paw that is offered you, stroke the head that leans against you. This is body language and it means more than words. Oh yes, these dogs can misbehave, or sometimes worse.'' Her eyes swept the class. ''Does this surprise you?''

Heads nodded.

''All right, let's say that your perfectly house-trained Cookie makes a puddle on your best carpet. Don't call Cookie. Go and get her. Show her what she has done, pointing your finger and looking displeased; give her the shakedown and let her have a moment to think things over while you mop up. Then put your arms around her and love her as if she were the dearest dog in the world, which she is. Chances are she won't wet again unless there's a physical problem; in that case you should take her to the vet. What if Laddie tends to bark at callers? Anticipate his behavior, and when you see him just thinking about barking, stop it before it happens.''

"How?''

"Get down to his level, take him by the scruff of the neck and give him a shakedown. Look at him sternly, point your finger at the door, shake your head and say, 'Don't you dare, don't you dare!' or something equally meaningful to him. And that brings up another point of behavior I want you all to be sure of: there is no excuse for aggression, *ever,* and you can curtail any tendency toward it by anticipating it and warding it off. Understand?''

One after another, heads nodded as each person became increasingly aware of all that the ownership of a Hearing Dog involved.

"You will soon learn of your dog's inner timing, and he will tell you in no uncertain way when he has to go out. But should you slip up and should it happen in a public place, be prepared. Always carry a plastic bag and a little scoop; dispose of the waste properly. It is the law, and both you and your dog must respect it.''

While the instructor was talking, one of the dogs named Emily had been inching herself toward the table and a doughnut that had been left there. Her nose could just reach it. She lifted a paw toward it, but before the tempting morsel was in her mouth, her owner saw her and drew in the leash sharply.

"Don't you dare," she said, removing Emily from the doughnut. "Don't you dare even to think of such a thing."

"Now what do you do?" the instructor asked.

"Love her."

"Yes, after the misbehavior has stopped and when you are sure she has learned her lesson. She won't try to sneak food again if you are on the watch."

While Emily was receiving her due of affection, the instructor turned to Willa. "What if Honey does something bad like getting up on the couch after you've told her not to?"

Willa looked puzzled and shook her head. She could not imagine Honey ever doing anything wrong; she could not see herself ever having to rebuke her.

"You'll say *off*, sternly, quickly, and you may have to use the shakedown just that once to impress her. Don't say the word *down*, since that's one of the commands she has learned. Say *off*, then reward her with praise. Tell her she's a good girl and that you love her."

The instructor looked around the group, again gathering everyone's attention. "In their enthusiasm your dogs may jump against you, and unless you nip that tendency, you'll have a real problem with your friends and anyone who comes to your house. All right, let's say that Jack's paws are suddenly on my chest and he is about to kiss me with that great lolling tongue. I'll bring my knee up against his chest with enough force for him to feel it and I'll say, *Don't jump.* The message will get through if you are quick enough.

Discipline is always done from love, and with love; but remember that sometimes love has to be tough.''

Five o'clock was feeding time for the dogs. Students were given bowls, shown where the food was, and told the amounts the dogs were accustomed to; then with bowls filled, they went to their rooms, closed their doors, and let the dogs eat. They were allowed time for a rest, then a walk.

Later, when the students gathered around the table for their supper, the dogs were given the down-stay command; some went under the table; some settled near chairs, tucking their noses between their paws. It did not appear necessary, but the instructor gave a precaution: "Never feed your dog from the table, and never give him rich food," he said. "Dogs function best on their own diet."

That night in her room, with Honey asleep at her feet, Willa reviewed the Basic Obedience sheet. The words had become familiar, and she read them with a smile of remembrance, recalling what Poppy had done without anybody taking the trouble to teach her anything, and what she had not done. All those commands, beginning with *heel,* would have been meaningless. Poppy had walked wherever she liked: ahead, behind, beside, and then she would disappear on adventures of her own. Hand signals? Poppy would have thought them a game, but with these dogs they were a form of language. Poppy would have liked the praise and the embrace that followed the exercises, whether she deserved them or not. But with these dogs, praise had to be earned, and then it was given lavishly.

She read a sheet with instructions about getting in and out of a car with your dog. Willa stared. Her father had taught her to drive years before she was old enough to have a license; but after the explosion, she had wondered if she would ever have a license, and she had talked herself into thinking she would never drive a car. Yet, something in her had kept the feel of a wheel in her hands, the place where her foot went for clutch or brake. Now, reading the instructions, she knew that she could have a car someday, for Honey would give her more than confidence; she would give her the warning necessary for decisive action in an emergency.

Willa imagined herself sitting at the wheel with Honey beside her, interested, alert, nose quivering. When traffic flowed normally, when signals were obeyed and road signs heeded, they would go freely about their business. If a siren sounded in the distance, Honey would hear it, put her front paws on Willa's right shoulder and keep them there until Willa had pulled to the side of the road and come to a halt. Once the fire engine, ambulance, or police car had zoomed by and traffic resumed its flow, Honey would sit upright on the seat again. It was the uncertainty that made Willa fearful, but a copilot could make a safe driver even safer. So into her future moved the shape of a car.

She began to think of other aids—a telephone with TDD, an instrument something like a typewriter that writes the message when the phone is answered; Honey would alert her to answer the phone. And there was something else that might be possible—a closed caption device to be attached to her television screen so she could read what she could not hear. But Honey would be in on this too. Willa would not leave the room wondering if she had turned the television off. If she had not, Honey would soon tell her and send her back to it. There were so many things Willa had told herself she would never be able to do. Now, *never* had become *perhaps*. She quivered with inner excitement. It was like the feeling of Christmas when she had to wait before she could unwrap a package whose contents she knew and longed for.

Willa sighed with happiness and glanced at Honey. The dog's presence in her room seemed to give a new meaning to life. They had communed together as two with a common bond, and though Honey was now asleep, head between paws and body relaxed, Willa's thoughts went on. She seemed to be looking at herself as she had not for a long time, facing herself without embarrassment or apology. True, she could not hear, but she could feel a nose when it pushed itself into her hand for attention; she could see eyes that looked into hers and spoke of things too deep for words; she could smell clean fur. What was it the psalmist had said? *Taste and see that the Lord is good.* Yes, she could taste and acknowledge the goodness. Four senses: she had consoled herself with that number for a long time, but it had taken a dog to help her realize how wonderful they could be.

She dropped her hand to run it over Honey's golden fur. One eye opened, the head lifted slightly, but when Honey saw that Willa had no command, no need, the head dropped back on the blanket. Honey's tail moved, a sigh twitched through her body, and she went back to sleep. Willa put her head down on her pillow. Once she had resigned her heart to loneliness; now it rested in companionship.

Chapter Three

"Auditory awareness" was the professional term, but "work on sounds" was more explicit, and this exercise was part of the lessons on obedience. It was individually done—one trainer, one student, one dog. Willa was taken into a large, sparsely furnished room. There was a cot with a table beside it and, some distance away, a chair and another table. The alarm clock Willa had brought with her was set, placed on the table by the cot, and she was told to get under the covers and pretend to be asleep.

The trainer sat down across the room and started to look at a magazine. Honey, free to do what she liked, investigated the room. Suddenly the alarm went off. Honey raced across the room, placed her paws on the cot, and tugged at the blanket. She kept tugging until Willa responded and sat up, wide awake. She told Honey what a good girl she was, and Honey's tail wagged with pleasure at her accomplishment and the treat that had been slipped to her.

A knocking sounded at the door. Honey, without so much as a glance at Willa, raced to the door, but she did not stay there. She ran back across the room to Willa, looked at her, and raced again to the door. She did this several times until she convinced Willa that the door should be opened. Someone stood there—another trainer—but Honey restrained her enthusiasm. She stayed beside Willa, gazing up at the one from whom her approval would come. When the smoke alarm went off, Honey looked startled. She hesitated a moment, then went to it, and raced back to Willa. "Honey, *tell*," Willa said, using the command word she had been told to say. Honey pushed against Willa and nudged her toward the door, indicating that this time they both must go out the door.

The trainer nodded. "Well done."

"I never seem to ask anything of Honey," Willa said.

"No, you don't ask, you tell, and that means for her to do it. The sounds we have just practiced are the first that every Hearing Dog learns. There are others, and some that are for particular people. Honey will alert you to any sound that could mean danger. It may mean nothing at all, but to her it is something you should know about. Cookie will be taught to respond to a baby's crying, since Cookie's owner has a small baby at home; Emily will respond to a kettle boiling. Tomorrow when we go out for a drive, you will see how Honey reacts to road sounds—a fire engine siren, an ambulance, a police car—and how she tells you of them.

The trainer smiled. "Some dogs have to be trained for very unusual sounds. In our last class there was a man from a part of Texas where rattlesnakes abound. His dog learned the warning sound made by a rattler and looked in its direction, but he did not go to it. It was the turn of the head that told the dog's owner there was something to be avoided in those tall grasses or that pile of rocks."

"However did you have a rattle handy?" asked Willa.

"We sent to Texas for one; so it was genuine enough. Is there something in your way of living that requires a certain sound?"

Willa could think of one: her own name. "Could Honey learn to respond to it when people call to me? So often they wonder why I don't answer."

"Of course," said the trainer. And they spent the rest of the time on that. First the trainer said *"Willa"* while pointing to Willa, then Willa said her name and pointed to herself. The exercise was repeated until Honey went easily to Willa when she heard her name said.

In a pause from working, Willa spoke of something that troubled her. "How will I know that I am using the right tone of voice when I talk to Honey?"

"She will let you know, for dogs respond best to a soft tone—their hearing is many times more acute than that of humans—and she is already used to yours and you have a gentle voice. But it will not be your voice alone that Honey will respond to. It will be your body language, what you do with your hands: caressing, rebuking, pointing a finger. It will be your facial expression: stern and set, smiling and tender. And your eyes! You were one of the first to discover the importance of eye contact." The trainer stood up. "Now, stay where you are. I'm going to leave, and we'll see if Honey remembers to tell you to come with me when she hears me say your name."

The trainer went to the door, started to open it, then turned back to call, "Willa—"

Willa saw the word on his lips. Honey, who was lying down and licking her paws, looked up, momentarily uncertain. When she heard the name again, she went to Willa, put her head in the outstretched hand, then looked toward the door. She put her paw on Willa's knee, conveying in her way that Willa was wanted. When she and Willa reached the door her reward came in words that charmed her. "Good girl, Honey. Oh, such a good girl!"

"Practice this often while you are here, and with your friends at home," said the trainer. "Your name is a new word for Honey, and it will take time for it to register. Never miss the chance to love, to let Honey know how needed she is and what good work she is doing."

That afternoon, the class had a health lesson. With their dogs beside them, they went to the kennels to see how a bath is given. The dog used in the demonstration seemed to enjoy every minute of the process. He had recently been given to the program by a couple living in Greece. They had found him lying on the side of a road outside Athens. His throat had been cut, and he had been left to die. They took him to the authorities and then to a veterinarian, who bandaged the wound and gave the necessary medication. No owner could be found; so the Americans were given the dog's papers and brought him home with them when they returned. Since they could not keep him, he was offered to the program. Medium in size, with smooth black hair and a one-sided smile, Kelly passed the test and endeared himself to everyone.

His training was slowed by the fact that he had to learn a new language. The Americans who rescued him had two small children; so Kelly had been matched to go to a home in the Midwest where there were two children. But that would not be for another month since he was in training for the next class. Kelly smiled his twisted smile and shook himself free of water when he was taken from the tub, and the lesson was over.

Back in the big room, the instructor showed the students how to keep their dogs' ears clean, swabbing them once a week, if necessary, with cotton dipped in an antiseptic lotion; how to check their eyes and their teeth; and how to keep their nails trimmed. They were told of the need for periodic visits to a veterinarian for essential shots such as parvovirus and rabies, and for heartworm tests, medication, and fecal examinations. "We know how to take care of ourselves," explained the instructor. "Your dogs are part of yourselves—they are your ears, and they deserve the best care you can give them."

Each day there was more to learn, more to experience, as the matched pairs became smoothly functioning teams. They were taken into stores and shopping malls. They went to restaurants; and when the students sat at tables, the dogs went under the tables. They were told to sit; then they were given the down-stay command, which would last through the meal. Leashes were rarely relied on, but they were still attached. The public library was accustomed to Seeing Eye Dogs, but now Hearing Dogs accompanied borrowers. As they passed a church, one student looked questioningly at a trainer, who assured her that wherever she went, her dog could go. "But, remember, it will be up to you to see that your dog is obedient to you at all times and that you are aware of your dog."

Always near, but deliberately unobtrusive since the dogs were no longer theirs, the trainers were ever watchful, sizing up the growing relationships and the matching that had been done. They saw points that would be taken up with the different owners. One woman needed to praise her dog more, another needed to allow more independence within the six-foot range, another more relaxation between commands. Even Honey should be permitted to be a bit of a rascal occasionally. Dogs were one answer to the problem of deafness, but they should not be expected to solve people's personal problems. They were not psychiatrists in fur coats but canines with differing temperaments and inborn tendencies that could be developed or sometimes needed to be corrected.

"Fun and games are as good for dogs as they are good for us," the instructor called. "So, off to the field for some baseball."

Sides were chosen and everyone available took part. Willa had not held a bat in her hands for years, but when the ball was pitched to her, she hit it hard. She ran to first base, Honey loping beside her, then to second, then to third and home. Players shouted. Dogs barked. Honey panted. Willa, seeing the excitement, reached down to stroke her dog. They each knew that something big had been accomplished. The game went on and there were other home runs, but Willa's first gave her a tingling of something that had been missing from her life for a long time.

"Play often with your dogs," the instructor was saying as they walked back to the house. "The more faithfully they work for you, the more sure they should be of the sheer joy it is to be with you. Run with them off lead in a park or field, whatever is near for you; throw a ball and let them bring it back so you can throw it again. And do dogs like Frisbees? Well, see for yourselves. It's all good exercise for you both and will keep you in training for the dog show next spring."

"Dog show?"

"Yes, it takes place every year, and we hope you'll all come back for it. Competition is keen, and there are all kinds of classes—for the Best Groomed, the Most Improved, Special Tricks, Best Tail Wag, and the crown of them all is Superdog. Even if you don't get a prize, it gives you a chance to show off your dog. Many sponsors come to the show, and that helps the program."

Finally the last day came. It was hard for the students to believe that the training was almost over, but they had the comforting feeling that they would keep in touch with each other and with the program. While learning to work with their dogs and relating to them, they had related to each other, and now they felt bonded as if by invisible leashes. Each day that added a stride toward independence marked a deepening of their friendship. Willa was not the only one who felt confidence replacing the anxiety that had overshadowed many of her days.

The ceremony that night was as solemn as it was challenging. Each student was given an orange leash and cape that were the right size and length for the particular dog, marked in large black letters: HEARING DOG. Each was given an ID card with a picture of the dog and the names of both dog and owner. The card was a proof of their graduation. "It is more than identification," the instructor explained. "It is a passport. As you have been told, your dogs are now certified by law to be with you wherever you go."

She held up a small booklet entitled *Legal Rights of Assistance Dogs*. "All fifty states have written this law into their statutes, and though the wording differs a little, it is basically the same. Here in Massachusetts, the law guarantees a person who is deaf or a person who is physically disabled the legal right to be accompanied by a specially trained dog in all public accommodations and on all public conveyances. It says clearly that no extra charge may be levied because of the presence of the dog guide and that the user—that's you and you and you—may be required to produce identification such as the card furnished by the school from which the dog was obtained. So always keep your ID cards at hand."

A collective smile passed over the group, and they stroked, patted, or embraced their dogs. Tails wagged. Cookie's went fast, others more slowly, and Honey's thumped on the floor. Something had happened that pleased her owner and that was all she needed to be pleased. Willa leaned toward her and whispered, "You may win the prize for the Best Tail Wag when it's time for the show." Honey's tail thumped harder.

"There's something more you should know," the instructor went on. "The Internal Revenue Service has decreed that any moneys expended on your dogs for licences, veterinarian fees, and food are all tax-deductible."

Again the collective smile, again the tails wagged and one tail thumped.

"The card you carry indicates that you as well as your dog have been professionally trained. What you both have is a privilege, and that is also a responsibility."

There were some in the group who read the words on the instructor's lips and saw the same in sign language. The sign for the word *responsibility* is a hand laid upon the shoulder where a burden is carried; in this case it was a burden proudly, gladly carried. Laws had been made and would be enforced so that a certain number of people deprived of hearing could, with their dog guides, move more freely in a hearing world. Seeing the words and the gesture, Willa leaned close to Honey and whispered into her ear, "Perhaps . . ." So much that had once seemed impossible seemed now to be within her reach.

Solemnity tired the dogs, and most of them were ready to flatten out in sleep, but the closing ceremony made the trainers even more enthusiastic. Relieved that one more class was safely launched, they were eager to reminisce about other dogs that belonged to the program.

"Remember Banjo?" one asked, and the others nodded. "He heard the smoke alarm before anyone else and went to wake up his owner and get her to the door. Then he went back, crawling along the floor, to rouse the other members of the household and get them out."

"And Bowen, remember what he did?"

Bowen, a former sheep dog, had been given to the program when his owner died. Used to herding cattle and sheep, he knew what numbers were in his care and never ceased his rounding until the last one was accounted for. When he was ten years old, he was placed in a home for the elderly, where he soon learned to respond not to one resident but to everyone in the house. The first time there was a fire drill he went to each room in turn and got its occupant to safety. Nothing deterred him until all were accounted for. The cook, knowing it was just a drill, did not leave the kitchen, but Bowen would not let her stay.

"Remember? She said she wouldn't have had a skirt to her name if she hadn't finally yielded to his tugging."

"Chico turned out to be a Superdog, but maybe that's because he got a college education."

"By association."

Chico was a chihuahua who had been kept secretly by some men in their college dormitory: fed, played with, and generally enjoyed. When the year was over, since he didn't belong to anyone in particular, he had been left behind. A custodian found him sitting all alone on a cot that had been stripped down to a mattress, looking as if he wondered what would happen next. The custodian took him to the shelter, and the shelter offered him to the program. He passed all the tests given him and went into training. Chico was smart, and his butterfly ears made him adept at identifying sounds. He had been matched to a woman who had lost her hearing because of a stroke and was confined to a wheelchair, and he spent most of his time in her lap. Light and swift, he would get to a door while the knock was still sounding or to the telephone's TDD while it was still ringing, then back and forth until his owner wheeled herself to the source.

"Chico writes good letters. We hear from him two or three times a year."

"Remember Flora?"

"Oh, poor Flora! We found her in a bus station. She had crawled into a corner behind some boxes and had just given birth to three tiny puppies. Two were already dead, one had a slim chance at life, and it was saved. Flora was so thin that her ribs almost stuck through her skin. She was so mangy and dirty you could hardly see what kind of dog she was. We took her to the shelter, where she was cleaned up and could nurse her one pup, then to the vet. She was fed, bathed, and cared for, and in a month she could have won a beauty contest. She had all the markings of a collie, but she was short haired. She responded to training as if she had been born to guide, and within a year she entered a new life as a certified Hearing Dog. She went to California. Who knows, she may be headed for Hollywood and a new career."

"Look at Ebony now."

"And remember *then*. Found wandering in a parking lot! When the owner was located he said he didn't want him and had turned him loose. Maybe someone would put the dog to sleep, but he couldn't pay for it. So we took Ebony."

"And Jack?"

"Oh, that's hard to believe. His people moved away. The neighbors saw the van and all the furniture loaded into it, the blinds in the house go down, and the FOR SALE sign go up. Next day they found Jack tied to a tree in the back yard. He was taken to the shelter and the owners were traced. They replied that they'd thought maybe someone else might want the dog—they didn't.''

Willa drew her hand across Honey's smooth head and looked into the golden eyes that returned her gaze. She didn't want to know about Honey's past. It was the present that mattered. Like the others, Honey had been given a purpose in life, work to do that needed doing and for which she had been trained. After a few moments, Willa lifted her head. They were talking about Molly, the little dog she had seen on television the night her life took a new direction.

''Molly may be small in size, but she does everything the others do and she has a special way that is all her own. You'll discover this with your dogs. They'll all develop something you've never taught them, and their company will give you added pleasure. Molly goes with one of us as a demonstration dog when we give talks to inform people about the program. After our work has been shown and explained, I say, 'If anyone would like to contribute a dollar or more, Molly will be glad to take it.'

''Someone is bound to respond, drawing a bill from purse or wallet and waving it in Molly's direction. She trots to the person, accepts it in her teeth, and trots right back to me with it. Then she looks expectantly around the room. One person after another wants to test her, and she is kept busy. The denomination doesn't matter; it's the crinkly sound that attracts her—perhaps its shape or color—and she is never fooled. You'll meet her next spring when you come back for the dog show and picnic.''

It was getting late, but the instructor had one more thought to leave with the graduates. "Just realize that a dog's life span is shorter than a human's. It may be that someday you will return for another dog. There will be one for you—one who needs your love and who has learned to give as you have learned to receive."

Later in her room, Willa hung the orange leash and cape over a chair and sat down on the bed. While Honey chewed on a rawhide bone, Willa read the final sheet of instructions that had been given out. Even though she was no longer a student but a graduate, she knew that education was a continuing affair and that it would be up to her to keep both Honey and herself in training by reintroducing the sounds and by bringing new ones into use. It would be work, for Honey was a working dog; but it could be done as a game too, and there would always be the reward in more than words. Privilege and responsibility—the words were interchangeable; but one belonged more specifically to Honey, the other to Willa.

The following morning, the dogs were taken for brisk walks to make sure elimination was complete before their journeys began in plane or bus or private car. Two proud owners were being called for by friends; two went off in the airport limousine; one had her own car and took the wheel with new confidence because of the copilot beside her.

The instructor and trainers stood on the steps of the building and watched them go. "Keep in touch. Write or phone if any problem arises, and remember that the outreach worker is always available for a visit. Keep the bonding of your leashes for another few days. The dogs will be in strange surroundings, and they will need to gain confidence from you. Good-bye, good-bye.''

Willa sat in the bus as she had two weeks ago, but now there was a comrade curled at her feet, and in her hand was an orange leash attached to a collar and a cape with words that would be honored wherever she went. Honey was giving her companionship and with it, independence. What she gave in return was love. Willa reached down to stroke the golden head, and a warm tongue licked her hand. Who needed to hear any words?

Chapter Four

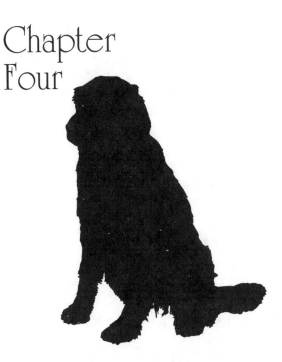

It was midafternoon when Willa turned the key in the lock and let herself and Honey into the apartment. The rooms had the reproachful air of having been closed too long, and Willa went through them, opening windows. Then she picked up the mail from where it had come through a slot in the door. There were bills to pay and letters to answer, reminding her of people she must visit to let them know she was back.

It will be easier to make calls now that Honey is with me, she thought. She checked the refrigerator to see what shopping she needed to do, and at the same time she introduced Honey to the kitchen. In her bedroom, she spread Honey's blanket on the floor by her bed, and Honey curled herself into a circle and settled down on it while Willa was unpacking.

"Not yet, Honey, there's much more to show you."
Willa startled herself with the realization that she now had
a companion to talk to. "And talk to your dogs often," she
could hear the instructor saying. "It's good for both of you.
It doesn't matter that one of you doesn't hear and the other
doesn't speak; it keeps avenues of communication open."

In the kitchen Willa filled a bowl with water that Honey
first sniffed, then lapped delightedly. From the kitchen, the
door opened to the little back yard, and they went out so
Honey could discover the area where she would be free of
the leash. She made the rounds, then returned to Willa and
the comfort of her presence in a world where everything
was new. Willa showed her the front door where a knock
would be a summons; then they returned to the bedroom,
and Willa showed Honey the alarm clock that would be
another summons.

Fully as important as their surroundings was getting to
know each other. At the training center they had taken each
other for granted; it might be different here. Willa sat down
in a low chair and called Honey to a position between her
knees so she could look into her eyes.

"You are Honey," she said slowly. "Honey. Honey."

At the sound of her name Honey quivered and started
to rise, expecting a command.

Willa pushed her down, then pointed to herself. "Willa." She repeated the name. Still pointing to herself she
said, "*Miss Macy*. Sometimes, Honey, that is what you will
hear people say, and both names mean me."

She left Honey and went across the room. Honey's eyes
followed her. "Honey, come to Willa." Honey bounded

across the room to stand beside her. She was rewarded with a warm "Good girl," then told to stay while Willa left her and recrossed the room. Bending low and clapping her hands, Willa said, "Honey, come to Miss Macy," and Honey did. The reward then was more than words, it was an embrace. Willa was pleased at Honey's response, but she knew that it was something they would have to work on constantly. There would be times, at the office especially, when Honey would need to answer to the more formal name.

Willa looked earnestly at Honey and said, "Wait, now, I'll be back." She left her and hurried to the nearby convenience store to do what shopping was needed. When she returned, Honey almost knocked her over in welcome.

"You'll have to get used to my leaving you sometimes, but on Monday we'll go to the office together," Willa told her. "No more work today, Honey. Let's just enjoy each other."

On Sunday afternoon Willa let the kettle in the kitchen boil longer than usual, and Honey heard it. Looking up from a careful licking of her paws she ran to the kitchen, saw the steam, and raced back to tell Willa. "Good girl," was her reward. "Thank you, Honey." Willa turned the stove off, made herself a cup of tea, and prepared Honey's supper. "Someday, Honey, we may have a telephone with TDD. Then you can tell me when to answer the phone. But they are very expensive; we'll have to wait."

Monday morning the alarm went off at six o'clock. Long before it ceased ringing, Honey's paws were on the bed and her nose was nuzzling Willa; then her long tongue began licking Willa's cheeks.

"That's enough," Willa said, stroking her, not sure whether to laugh or cry at Honey's enthusiasm.

Honey, knowing she had accomplished her duty, went to the back door and put her nose to the crack. Willa let her out into the fenced yard, then went to shower and dress. By the time they were both ready for the day, breakfast was at hand—a bowl of cottage cheese and a biscuit for Honey, while Willa sat at the table with coffee and toast. "Was the coffee all that bad at the training center?" she asked herself, for never had coffee tasted so good.

It was only a few blocks to the Locke Insurance Company, and Willa generally walked; but this time she took the bus. "Use the privilege that is yours," she could hear the instructor saying, "and remember, you're pioneers in this field."

Standing at the bus stop, pocketbook in her right hand, Honey's leash in her left, she watched as the big gray bus came around a corner and drew to a stop. The door opened part way and the driver leaned toward her. "It's nice to see you back, Miss Macy, but dogs aren't allowed on. Sorry."

Willa held Honey's leash toward him and pointed to the words on Honey's cape. HEARING DOG was clearly marked in black letters. "This dog is," she said. She reached into her purse for her ID card, which she had been taught to have ready when needed.

The driver glanced at it, looked puzzled, then smiled and opened the door its full width. "This is a first time for me and for the company too. It's something to have a first on a Monday morning. Should mean good luck for the rest of the week."

What he said meant no more to Willa than it did to Honey; what mattered was that the steps could be mounted and there was a seat next to the door.

Willa usually arrived early at the office, but today others were there before her. Several of the staff standing near the door made themselves a welcoming committee. Hands reached out, first to grasp Willa's, then to stroke Honey's head.

"Isn't she beautiful!"

"Aren't you lucky!"

"First dog ever to be in the office!"

The remarks passed over Willa like a spring breeze, but the smiles gave her the assurance of acceptance; and on her desk was a vase of flowers and a dog biscuit tied with a pink ribbon.

One of the men stood before her and said, "When you are settled, Mr. Locke would like to see you and your friend."

Willa nodded. "We'll go in a moment." She took only long enough to put her purse away and gather up her notebook and pencil.

Mr. Locke rose and held out his hand to her. "You've been missed, but there wasn't a person in the office who was not delighted at what you were doing, and they have all had a part in it."

Honey, standing beside Willa, was composed but attentive; and when Mr. Locke looked down at her, she solemnly lifted her right front paw and placed it against his leg.

"Well mannered, isn't she?" he commented.

"More than that." There was much Willa wanted to say, but it was Monday morning. She had been away a month and there was work to be done.

"These reports, Miss Macy, are ready to be typed. I'll be glad to have them before you leave this afternoon." He faced her directly, speaking clearly and slowly as he went over them.

"You shall," she replied. "My fingers are itching to get back to the keys." She took the papers in her right hand, gave Honey a command, a pull on the leash, and they were out the door.

"Oh, Miss Macy, just one thing more—" Mr. Locke stopped, realizing he was talking to a disappearing back. He turned to his desk. Why was it so hard to remember that she did not understand words directed to her unless she was face to face? He looked up to see her standing beside his desk.

"You have something more for me?"

"Yes, I— I—" Mr. Locke looked puzzled. "How was it you heard me call you?"

"I didn't. Honey blocked my way. She wouldn't go forward until I turned and came back to your office."

"Smart dog; beginning to show the worth of our investment. Yes, Miss Macy, I have another letter, a personal one. I'd like you to do it today. Take it down now, if you please."

Willa's notebook and pencil were ready. She was used to Mr. Locke's dictation, used to keeping her eye on his lips and trusting shorthand to her fingers.

"Denis Talcot, 64 Sycamore Street," she read back to Mr. Locke. "I am glad to second your application for custodial work at St. Martin's. You have already received your instructions, and a check will be mailed to you the first of every month."

Mr. Locke listened while Willa read, then he nodded, but he seemed inclined to talk. "He's a nice young fellow—getting his Masters in Social Work. Wants to do something with juvenile delinquents. In my day we called them bad boys." Mr. Locke looked away and Willa did not understand all he was saying, but his comments had nothing to do with the content of the letter.

"I'll do it now, Mr. Locke, and bring it back to you for signing when I have the reports ready." She closed her notebook, gave Honey a signal, and the two left the room.

At lunch time Willa took Honey out for a brief walk. Returning, she tied Honey to her desk and went to the cafeteria. People crowded around her, asking questions.

"Can Honey roll over if you tell her to?"

"Why?"

"Show how clever she is."

"She'll show that in other ways. Honey is a working dog."

"Will she sit up if I give her some dog candy?"

"Honey doesn't beg for treats, but she is rewarded by them for special behavior."

"Doesn't she do any tricks?"

"She'll do what she's trained to do—alert me to certain sounds. A Hearing Dog doesn't do tricks. You'll see."

What they did see, and it happened several times during the day, was that when someone approached Willa from the side or from behind, she turned to face the person and was often the first to begin a conversation. Honey had given her a cue.

The office closed at four. Willa walked home, knowing she had just time enough to go by the Town Hall and secure a dog license for Honey. On the clerk's desk she put the ID she and Honey shared and Honey's vaccination certificate. She was prepared to explain her request, but the clerk was ready for her.

"Mr. Locke told me you'd be in, and I've set aside a special license for your dog. Now, give me her name, breed, and age, and I'll clip the license onto her collar. She's one in a hundred, you know."

"I do know. Her name is Honey, she is a golden retriever, spayed female, three years old." Willa looked at the license, which was shaped like a little bone. The number on it was One. She smiled, realizing they had both been given something to live up to.

Honey did not seem impressed by her distinction, but she relished the fondling the clerk gave her.

"Likes affection, doesn't she?"

"It's her life." Willa opened her purse to pay the fee.

The clerk shook her head. "Seeing Eye Dogs and Hearing Dogs pay no fee. The town is honored by their presence, and Honey is the first of her kind here as well as being Number One."

Willa thanked the clerk, and Honey offered her right paw, then they went on their way.

Returning from the cafeteria on Wednesday, Willa discovered one of the staff feeding Honey half a hamburger, which Honey was devouring with gusto.

"I want her to like me," was the explanation, "and she did look so hungry."

"Honey has her own food," Willa said, "and she eats at her own times. Giving a dog tidbits is not the way to win affection. Your hands stroking her will tell her you appreciate her. If she offers you her paw, accept it. That's her evidence of friendship."

One of the young messengers came up to Willa, hand in his pocket. Honey looked at him, then put her head down between her paws and looked as if she was going to sleep.

"What kind of dog is that, anyway? I've been buzzing this thing until it's nearly worn out, and all she does is look at me."

"Let Honey see you put it on my desk and set it to go off in a few minutes, then go back to your work. But be sure she sees you."

Five minutes later, the buzzer went off with a sound far louder than when it had been in the boy's pocket. Honey stood up, looked at it, put a paw on Willa's knee, looked at Willa, then at the boy who was standing near a file cabinet. Willa picked up the gadget and went to the boy with it.

"See? She alerted me to the sound, which is what she is supposed to do; then she looked from me to you because she saw you put it on my desk and connected you with the sound."

The boy's teasing expression was washed out by admiration. "She really does think, doesn't she! What do I do now?"

"Tell her she's a good girl. Stroke her; let her know you're friends."

Even though Willa had been outspoken about Honey's diet, there were still some who could not resist feeding her with morsels from their lunches. A paper cup of coleslaw was offered to Honey, and, partly because she was polite and partly because she could not resist attention, she ate it. It was not long before she went over to a corner of the room and relieved herself of it. When she returned to her place beside Willa's desk, Willa thought she saw a slightly smug look about Honey, as if she could be relied on to handle things in her own way.

Willa had not heard the retching sounds but her nose told her all she needed to know. She saw what had happened and cleaned it up as quickly as possible, glad that she could not hear the comments that were being made. When she returned from the washroom, Mrs. Golding went up to her and said, "If that dog is so smart, she should know what doesn't agree with her and refuse it."

Willa reached down to stroke Honey. "With dogs we do what is possible within a certain range. Honey has had only intermediate training. If she had gone on for advanced, that is one of the lessons she would be taught—to refuse any food except what comes from the hand of her owner."

Mrs. Golding was determined to have the last word. "I'm going to speak to Mr. Locke about having a dog in a business office. Some of us have allergies to animal hair."

On Friday afternoon when Willa delivered some reports to Mr. Locke, he asked how people were taking to the presence of a dog.

"Some people understand dogs more than others," Willa said.

"It's up to you, of course, to see that Honey is under control at all times."

"Two words were made very clear to us, Mr. Locke, when we were in training—privilege and responsibility. Neither Honey nor I will let the program down, or betray your confidence in us."

"It's always 'we' isn't it?" Mr. Locke asked with a smile.

Willa smiled back. "Yes, of course. Honey and I are a team."

She went back to her desk to cover her typewriter and put some papers away. The others had gone, but that was not unusual; she was often the last person to leave. Honey looked at her intently, then raced out to the hallway and down to the door marked *Ladies,* back to Willa, then back again to the door.

"Honey, that's not the way we go out. Come." Willa picked up the leash and went toward the front door, but Honey had no intention of going that way. To humor her, Willa went toward the restroom; then she saw that the door was being beaten on so hard that it was shaking. Obviously someone was knocking. Willa put her hand on Honey's head. "Someone's trying to get out. Why didn't I trust you? We're here," she called. "I'll see if I can loosen the lock from the outside; it's always been tricky."

Working with the aid of a nail file, Willa finally eased the lock open, and out plunged Mrs. Golding. Her face was streaked with tears, distorted by panic.

"Honey heard you knocking. That's one of her sounds," Willa said, trying to calm the distraught lady. "She thought you wanted to get in."

"Why, I might have been here all weekend!" Mrs. Golding half-sobbed. Still trembling, she looked at Honey and suddenly dropped to her knees and put her arms around the dog. "You blessed animal," she said. She looked up at Willa, "What did you say her name was?"

"Honey."

"She's that all right. Can't I give her something to show her how grateful I am?"

"Your affection is doing that."

"The door—what happened?"

"It looks as if the bolt got jammed. I'll leave a note for the janitor to fix it when he comes in on Monday morning."

Chapter Five

Willa did not set the alarm for Saturday morning, but she woke up not long after her usual time. She glanced across the room to the corner where Honey had her nest. Curled up into a round ball, she was sleeping soundly. Willa luxuriated in a long, slow stretch and the realization that she did not have to get up at a prescribed time. They had both been tired and had earned the right to sleep in.

Willa was always in a state of tension at work, having to be ready to give "ear" to anyone who came to her desk and make an effort not to be startled. This week it had been easier since Honey invariably nudged her knee at the sound of approaching footsteps. Then Willa could look up and be ready to face friend or colleague. Alerted, it was possible to smile, knowing that someone was coming to her for something she could do.

Honey had been very attentive every day, and this morning she had good reason to relax. Willa snuggled into the bed clothes and went back over the week. Honey had done well enough for her to send a good report back to the program. That first occasion when she responded to "Miss Macy" and returned Willa to Mr. Locke proved something to him. And last night's experience with Mrs. Golding spoke for itself.

Honey began to stir, uncurling herself, rising and stretching slowly, shaking herself and stretching again; then she looked across the room. Willa's eyes were open and gazing at her; then it seemed as if Honey suddenly realized there was work to do. She leaped across the room and started licking Willa's face, stopping only long enough to peer at the alarm clock on the table.

"It's all right, Honey; this is the day we have to ourselves."

The orange leash and cape remained on a rack near the door. After breakfast Willa went to her desk to catch up on long-neglected mail, and Honey went back to her nest. "That's right, Honey; when there's nothing else to do, rest," Willa told her. "We never know when something might call us back into action."

After an hour, Willa was prompted to go to the bedroom, and there she saw Honey working away methodically at a project of her own. She had very nearly removed the zipper from the outer cover of the pillow that was her nest. "Honey, what are you doing!" Willa exclaimed.

Honey looked up, wagged her tail, and went back to her zipper.

"No, no, you mustn't do that." The words rose in Willa, but she did not say them.

For reasons known only to Honey, the zipper was being removed from the outer covering. The inner pillow that held cedar shavings was intact, stoutly sewed, and seemed to hold no interest. Willa told herself she would get another zipper, or perhaps replace it with buttons. Honey, so used to working, probably had to find something to do, and a little tooth testing had appealed to her. Words from one of the trainers echoed in Willa's mind: "Every dog has to be a bit of a rascal now and then."

After a while Willa said, "That's enough," in a tone that was anything but stern. Honey left the tangled threads and the length of zipper, and went to stand beside her, looking up into her face, licking her hand; everything in her was ready to respond.

Later that morning they had a practice session, and Willa ran through some of the sounds to which Honey had been trained to respond—not the door knock, which had already been well tried, but the timer in the kitchen, the tea kettle, and the smoke alarm that could be activated by holding a flashlight close to it. Honey went through them all, dutifully but not enthusiastically, as if she knew they were not for real.

Willa, always looking for ways to extend her range, left a water tap running in the cellar while Honey was out in the yard. Honey paid no attention until she settled into her nest for a second sleep and Willa started to lose herself in a book. Watching surreptitiously, she saw Honey lift her head, cock it, then go to the door that led down to the cellar.

Honey stayed beside it but did not nose it open to go down and investigate.

After a few moments of obvious uncertainty over a sound new to her, she went to Willa and put a paw on her knee to get her attention. Once Willa looked up, she went back to the cellar door and waited. Willa responded to the signal and went downstairs to turn off the dripping tap. When she returned she embraced Honey. "Good girl," she said over and over. Dripping water was one more sound she could add to Honey's list.

The letters on her desk told Willa of things she should do and people she should see, but she put off answering them. The week at the office had given her and Honey all the new experiences and people they needed; more could wait. Ever since she had been deaf, Willa's tendency had been to withdraw, to retreat into herself. It was an effort to be with people, to be watching lips and then replying the best she could. Often the effort drained her of energy that should have gone into sociability. Today, this weekend, was for Honey and herself, but it was too nice a day to stay indoors. She called to Honey, put the cape on her, and fastened the leash to her collar. Together they went to the nearby park for a walk.

There, where the grass was green, she gave Honey her freedom, but Honey took it warily and soon returned to Willa for the assurance of the leash and her company. A few people spoke to Willa, attracted by Honey, whose friendliness was evident. Seeing the words HEARING DOG, they asked questions. Willa found her desire to withdraw diminishing when she could talk about Honey.

On the way home she passed St. Martin's church and saw someone raking leaves. Mr. Locke's words recurred to her. "Nice young fellow." Willa had imagined someone not much more than a boy, but this was a tall man, raking as if he knew what he was about and with a vigor that implied there must be no leaf left on the lawn when Sunday morning came. A young woman emerged from the church and went up to him. He put down the rake and the two talked together, even laughed. Willa saw it all without turning her head; she had become adept at using the corners of her eyes. She quickened her pace. Honey, loving people and jollity, gave a little pull at the leash as much as to say, "Why don't we join them?" Willa drew the leash in tightly. "Honey, heel," she said in a firm tone, and at the next intersection she turned down the street that would take her home and away from St. Martin's.

Pictures lingered in her mind long after she got back to her apartment; long after she had given Honey her daily grooming; long after she had had supper and settled down to read a book. She kept seeing the busy young man, joined by the pretty young woman, the way he had put down his rake to talk with her, the way she had said something to make him laugh. What had they been talking about? What were they laughing about? Had he gone back to leaf raking or gone into the church with her? Then loneliness closed in around Willa like a wall. It was an old feeling and she knew it well, so well that she had learned to accept it. After a while it usually went away, like a pain, but this time it did not. She put her head in her hands and started to cry. Tears came in a flood and wracking sobs shook her shoulders.

The sobs were audible to Honey, who went to Willa's side as readily as if she had been called. She waited patiently, but there was no response. Honey's soft warm tongue began lapping Willa's hands, then her cheeks as they were uncovered; then she looked into Willa's eyes.

"Nobody taught you the sound of a sob," Willa said, when she felt herself in control, "but now you know. Now you know."

* * * * *

During the next few weeks Honey was acknowledged to be a full-fledged member of the office staff. She sat most of the time by Willa's desk, but there were moments when she made brief visits to others, especially to Mrs. Golding, whose fondling was always lavish and who made no mention of any allergy. Honey's retriever instinct was in evidence when wastepaper aimed at a basket missed its mark. She would rise quietly, pick it up and return it to the sender, standing with her tail wagging and an expectant look. Everyone knew now that the look asked for a show of affection, and it was readily given.

It had been impressed on Willa at the training center that a Hearing Dog owner had the opportunity to make such dogs and their work known. Willa's long-time reluctance to face strangers was being overcome because of Honey, and for the sake of other Honeys and the people who needed them she braved new encounters. One such was the Post Office, which had a sign on its door saying NO DOGS ALLOWED EXCEPT SEEING EYE DOGS. Mustering her courage one Saturday morning, she went in with Honey and asked to see the postmaster.

When she was ushered into his office, she placed herself opposite him, where the light was on his face. She introduced Honey, displaying the harness and leash with their descriptive words, showed her ID, and requested that the sign on the door include Hearing Dogs. The postmaster started to demur, but Honey, as if on cue, put her right paw on his knee and looked at him with eyes that he later said could melt a stone.

"Are there any other such dogs in town, Miss Macy?"

"Not yet, but there are two people who need them."

The postmaster asked more about the program, and Willa found herself doing what had never been easy for her to do—talking with someone she scarcely knew.

"We'll take care of that sign, and soon," were the postmaster's final words as he stroked Honey's head.

Willa left, cheered by the feeling that one mission had been accomplished.

She repeated the process at the bank and at the library, but they were places where she was known, and recognition made it easier. The supermarket should have been next on her list, but she dreaded the confrontation. Her shopping had always been done at the convenience store near her apartment where she was well known.

A time for the supermarket came sooner than she expected. At the end of the first month when paychecks were delivered, Willa was surprised to see two envelopes on her desk, one with Honey's name on it. She opened it and found a certificate for $25 to purchase Honey's favorite food at the Sunnyside Supermarket.

"Oh, but I've never gone there!" Willa exclaimed.

The office staff congratulated Honey, but Willa had misgivings. The store was so big, often crowded, and she knew none of the clerks. Willa shook her head with uncertainty.

Mrs. Golding spoke up brightly. "I'm going there tonight on my way home. Let's go together."

Willa smiled, the rare smile that said more than words. She was touched that people wanted to help her. Perhaps people would always have been willing, but she had held them at bay. Embarrassment, timidity, diffidence had driven her deep into herself, but she was beginning to shake such feelings off the way Honey shook rain from her coat when she came in out of the wet. "Thank you," she murmured.

It was not easy in the supermarket. Many people looked askance at Willa, and there were obviously those who felt that a place where food was sold was no place for a dog. Willa kept her ID card in one hand and the leash in the other, while Honey trotted next to the grocery cart. Mrs. Golding, walking beside them with her own cart, was ready to do battle if needed or extol something so remarkable as a dog who heard for its owner.

That night when Willa put away her purchases in the kitchen, Honey watched intently. Then Willa looked as directly at Honey as she liked to have people look at her. "Honey, you are giving me confidence. I'm doing things I've shied away from, dreaded doing, for years and years. Thank you!"

It was not the words so much as the embrace that made Honey wag her tail.

56

Assurance was coming to Willa in many ways, through many avenues, but it was shaken late one night. She was reading, curled up on the couch with Honey at her feet. Honey stirred and stood up, glanced around the room, then went to the window that looked out on the back yard. Returning to Willa, she nuzzled her, then went back to the window, nosing intently. Willa felt a runnel of fear. This was something she had been advised about during training. The dogs were schooled to warn of any unusual sound, even a possible intruder.

The window was closed, the shade was down, and no one could see in, but Willa couldn't help wondering whether anyone could get in. She spoke sternly to Honey, pointed to her place on the floor, and told her to lie down, but Honey would not leave the window. Finally Willa yielded. Approaching the window, she said in a firm voice, "Who's there?" and let the shade go up.

Oh! It was only a shutter that had come loose and was banging against the window frame. A minute before, she felt weak with fear; now she felt weak with relief and wanted only to sit down and laugh at herself. But she knew that Honey would give her no peace until the noise was stopped; so she opened the window and pushed the shutter back onto its hook. Then she sat down on the floor and hugged Honey. "Thank you," she said. "That's another one of your sounds, isn't it?"

* * * * *

The next week, their approach to the park for the usual Saturday morning romp took them close to St. Martin's church. Willa was careful to walk on the sidewalk across the street from the church, but she did not see the "nice young fellow" this time.

Perhaps, leaves having all fallen, he was working inside the church. She was torn between wanting to see him and fearful as to what she would say if they ever did meet. Honey was often the one to make the introduction, but Willa did not feel easy about this meeting. She had an advantage in that she knew his name—Denis Talcot—remembered easily from the letter Mr. Locke had dictated. If they did meet, she would have to tell him her name, then point to the words on Honey's leash.

Safely past St. Martin's without an encounter, she met a little girl in the park who was tossing a Frisbee into the air and racing gleefully after it. Spying the dog, the child ran up to Willa. "What's your dog's name?"

"Honey."

"Does she like to play Frisbee?"

"I don't know." Willa looked at Honey, who was nosing the disc, tail wagging, and tongue alternately licking the little girl's hand and the Frisbee. Honey looked at Willa. Pleading was in the dog's eyes, her stance, her whole being. "Try it," said Willa, and unhooked the leash.

The child tossed the red disc into the air. It went high but not far, and Honey ran fast, then leaped to catch it. She danced about with it in her mouth and returned it to Willa; so Willa threw it. It went higher, but not too high for Honey to catch it, wheel herself about, and return it again to Willa.

"She knows she belongs to you, doesn't she?" the little girl asked. She knelt on the ground with her arms around

Honey, her eyes on Willa. "Why didn't you answer me when I called to you the first time Honey caught it?"

"Because I didn't hear you. I have to see your lips making words. My ears don't tell me things, but my eyes do." Willa pointed to the words on the leash. "Honey is my ears."

The child's eyes widened. "Words on lips?" She looked closely at Willa as if she might see words taking actual shape when Willa spoke. "Words," the girl repeated with new respect. Always before, spoken words had been like fluff from a dandelion that disappeared in the distance or released balloons that were soon lost to sight. Now she knew they were shapes that could be seen by some people.

"Will you tell me about the words you see when my lips are moving? My name is Rosey." Now she spoke slowly, wondering what it looked like on her lips.

"And my name is Willa."

Rosey heard but could not see the word, just a mouth opening, lips moving.

Sensing her dismay, Willa smiled comfortingly. "It doesn't happen all at once. People have to study hard to learn speech reading, and some of it is guess work."

"Tell me more. This is like a story."

There was a bench near; so they went over and sat on it. Honey nestled at Willa's feet, settling the golden head on her knee, restful but alert.

It had been a long time since Willa had thought about storytelling, but she remembered what it had meant to her as a little girl when her father answered her demand for a story. So she told Rosey about the work that Honey did and explained that there were other dogs training to be ears for deaf people. She showed Rosey some simple signing—the hand on the shoulder that meant *burden,* the arms lifted high that meant *elation.* The hand closed except for one finger held against the chest that meant *I,* then the hand with one finger pointing outward that meant *you.*

Rosey was fascinated. "This is fun," she said, shaping her lips carefully and moving her hands. "Using more of me makes talk more interesting."

Willa nodded, recalling that the instructor had taught them about using body language with their dogs: the eyes, the facial expression, the finger pointing, the hand widespread in command, curved in caress.

"How do you sign *love?*"

Willa showed her, arms crossing chest, hands just below the shoulders. "It's so simple, almost the way it feels," she said.

"Is there a book in the library that could tell me about this kind of talking?" asked Rosey.

"Many books."

Rosey's face brightened. "Maybe next time we meet I'll have some words for you."

Soon they parted, Rosey picking up her Frisbee and skipping off, Willa and Honey walking on their way. Suddenly Honey stopped short and looked toward the child who was calling back to them. Willa turned and waited. Rosey came running up, her face filled with contrition.

"I'm sorry, I forgot. I just wanted to tell you that I'm going to the library on my way home to get one of those books."

Willa had an almost uncontrollable desire to put her arms around Rosey and hug her, but she had been locked within herself too long to be easily demonstrative with anyone but Honey. Rosey had no such inhibition. She flung her arms around Willa's waist. "This has been the best day ever!" She paused, then signed "I love you" and raced off across the grass.

"You are making things happen, Honey." At the sound of the familiar voice now directed to her, Honey licked the back of Willa's hand. Willa felt so lighthearted that she walked right past St. Martin's without even troubling to cross to the other side of the street.

Chapter Six

One Saturday morning Willa opened the kitchen door to call Honey in from her usual time in the yard, but no Honey came. Willa called more insistently. She went out and looked all around the small space; then she saw to her dismay that a gate near the house had been left open. Honey had evidently walked through it and out into the world.

For an agonizing moment Willa thought of the possibilities. Stolen? No. No one would take a dog clearly identified as having been trained for a distinct purpose. Curiosity? Well, that would be normal in an animal. Adventure? Perhaps; but nothing really made sense to Willa. Considering her breed, her training, her bonding with her owner, it was unlikely that Honey would go far on her own. Yet at the training center Willa had been told that this might happen for a variety of reasons. A dog could be as subject to boredom as a human and act on its own initiative.

Willa knew what she should do: let the police know and alert the neighborhood; but without a telephone, that meant making personal calls, which she dreaded doing. Besides, she was not ready for the day; Saturdays moved at a different pace than other days, and she had not dressed yet. But there was no time to lose. Forego her shower, forego her breakfast, pull on some clothes and get out. "Honey," she said, as if to test her voice, knowing that calling would do little good since her voice had such a limited range. Anxiety turned to anguish and got into her fingers, causing them to fumble as she tried to tie the laces on her shoes, and one lace after another knotted.

What if Honey had been stolen, maybe even picked up by a car that was now miles away to nowhere? What if she had been hit and was lying on the road dead, or worse, had been injured and had wandered off to suffer and die as animals did? What if she was kidnapped and was being held for a ransom, tied in some dark and lonely shed? Would she cry pitifully or bark impatiently? Willa couldn't bear to imagine any more. All that could happen flashed through her mind as her fingers struggled to loosen the knots and finally tie her shoes. Yet beyond everything was Honey's sweetness. Wouldn't that save her from cruel treatment? Perhaps, but not from a speeding car. Anguish gave way to resolve, and Willa knew that she would do whatever had to be done, for Honey's sake. She put on her coat, picked up Honey's orange leash, and went to the front door.

As she opened it, she was startled to see a young man there, with Honey beside him.

"Oh!" Willa's mouth was so dry that almost no sound came from it.

"I've been ringing your bell and knocking for the last five minutes. I thought no one was home."

Honey threw herself against Willa, whose hands were ruffling her coat, pressing her close to make sure she was real.

"Oh, thank you, thank you!" Her voice was faint but returning. "If Honey isn't in the house, no bell or knock is heard. She is my ears. Where was she?"

"Snuffling in the shrubbery around St. Martin's."

"You're Denis Talcot, aren't you?" Willa asked, as relief about Honey swept away her feeling of awkwardness with strangers.

"Yes, how did you know?"

"A couple of months ago, Mr. Locke dictated a letter to you that I typed. I've seen you working around St. Martin's. Won't you come in?"

Denis held out his hand. "You're Willa Macy."

"How did you know?"

"Everybody in town knows of you, but very few people seem to know you."

Honey stood between them, looking from one to the other like a hostess who has at last achieved an introduction she had long been wanting to make. Then, her mission accomplished, she raced in circles of abandonment and joy around the room.

Denis followed Willa, and she gestured to a chair where the light would be on his face; then she sat down too. "You speak as if you heard me."

"I see you."

"You're reading my lips?"

Willa nodded. "Speech reading it's called, but it's really speech speculation. Only about thirty per cent of all words are visible on lips. There's a lot of guess work, and it's helped by expression and gestures."

"That's real communication, isn't it, because it involves so much of the person? Words aren't everything."

A smile flooded Willa's face; it was so rare to be understood and so soon.

Honey took herself off to another part of the room and settled down. Conversation began between Denis and Willa, each knowing something about the other and reaching for more.

Looking toward Honey, Denis asked, "Is that all right, what she's doing?"

Willa turned around to see. Honey had pulled a cushion from the couch, one that had an outer cover held in place by a zipper. Carefully, methodically, she was working her way around the zipper with the clear intent of removing it from the cushion.

Willa laughed. "That's her one misdeed, but now I call it her hobby. She's so well trained and naturally polite, she has never chewed or done anything to merit disapproval except this. I've remonstrated with her, pleaded with her, but somehow I haven't been able to scold her. Removing zippers is her thing, and I've decided to let her do it. That one is, I think, the last one available to her. I'm careful not to leave any of my clothes that have zippers within her reach.''

It was Denis's turn to laugh. ''Almost every dog has some idiosyncrasy,'' he said. Then he realized by Willa's expression that the word was a difficult one and he amended it. ''Some little way. Each to his own.'' They laughed together. Honey had broken the ice between them, and conversation flowed easily.

An hour later when Denis left, they knew enough about each other to provide the basis for a growing friendship. Willa knew that Denis's parents had been divorced when he was ten and that from then on until his college years he had lived a divided life—the week with his mother, the weekend with his father. His dog, Pundit, a collie, was the only thing of which he could be sure, for Pundit went with him always.

''Where is Pundit now?''

''He came to the end of his days last summer,'' Denis replied, as quietly as if he might be speaking of a sunset that marked the end of a day. ''He was sixteen.''

''Last summer,'' Willa repeated, and her heart lurched toward Denis, ''just when Honey was coming into my life.''

Denis knew as much about Willa as most people in the town did. She was a shy young woman, who was profoundly deaf. She had been a good student in school, but after the accident that took her hearing she had gone away to special schools for speech reading, as well as formal studies. During those years she had been protected by her parents. Then one had died and a year later the other. All she had left of the past was the old dog Poppy; all she could give to the future were the secretarial skills she had acquired. Living alone, she had become more withdrawn.

He told her about his graduate study and explained why he wanted to work with delinquent juveniles. "Some of us in high school made up a gang, and we did things that we knew weren't right. We didn't know why we did them. It took me a long time to realize that a prank could lead to a tragedy. There was one; it's haunted me all my life. I'd like to tell you . . ." he turned away, his lips still moving.

Willa leaned toward him and put her hands on his cheeks, turning him back to face her so she could see what he was saying. "Please, I want to know what it is you are going to do."

"Work with young people, find out why they choose to go the wrong way, and head them into the right way," said Denis. "What is delinquency anyway? There's a terrible longing behind it, some kind of misunderstanding, some lack of realization of consequences. Pundit did more for me in those years than any person. I could talk to him, and he never answered back. He just looked at me, and I knew I had to find my own answers."

Willa smiled, remembering Mr. Locke's comment: "Juvenile delinquents. In my day we called them bad boys."

When it was time to go, Denis lingered at the door as if he found it hard to leave. "On the first Monday evening of the month I sort the bundles and boxes of clothes that people bring to St. Martin's for World Service," he said. "Some are in beautiful condition, others deserve" —he shrugged— "obliteration is the only decent word. Come over some evening. There just might be an old pair of zippered jeans that Honey could have some fun with.''

''Will you let me help?''

''I'd welcome help. It's a lonely job.''

Willa watched him as he went down the street. *Lonely.* It was a word she knew all too well. So he was lonely too. Perhaps everyone was lonely at times without being able to talk about it.

She went over to Honey, who was sleeping soundly beside her finished task. The cushion was without its cover; the zipper lay curled beside it. Honey's eyes opened when Willa stroked her. ''You always do such a neat piece of work.'' Willa picked up the zipper and put it in the waste basket; the cushion she tossed back to the couch. Then they went out to the yard to play ball, Willa throwing nimbly and Honey retrieving expertly.

After the game, Willa led Honey to the gate, now securely fastened. She took Honey's nose between her hands, looked her in the eyes, and shook her head. Freeing one finger she pointed to the gate and said no as firmly as she could. ''We never go out that way.''

It was the pointing finger and the severe look that got through to Honey. Her eyes, so merry and melting, grew mournful; her tail, so constantly in motion, drooped.

* * * * *

Willa's frequent reports back to the program conveyed the assurance that she and Honey were doing all right; so the outreach worker deferred her visit. When she came, she looked with approval at the team they made.

"Honey's coat is handsome; that's because of the right food and daily grooming. Any problems?"

"No, not really. We don't practice all the sounds every day; we alternate for the sake of surprise, and we've been discovering some of the new ones. But tell me about Jack and Cookie, Ebony, Laddie, and Emily. How are they?"

As the worker talked about the dogs Willa had known at the training center, even Honey tilted her head at the sound of the familiar names. "You were an unusual class and are all doing well," the instructor concluded. "The class before you had to return a dog."

"Whatever happened?" It was hard for Willa to imagine how a relationship could fall apart after the bonding and the weeks of training.

"It's not without humor." The instructor's grin put Willa at ease. "Bosco was one of the best dogs we ever trained, a beagle-cocker mix, which is good when you get the best of both breeds. He passed all his tests, behaved admirably in training, and acted as if his owner was the only person in the world."

"And then?"

"Once he got to his new home he was the darling of the family. But he answered no bells; he let kettles boil dry; he was oblivious to knocks. He made it quite clear that he was not a working dog; he intended to enjoy his life. The family loved him, but a dog who could hear for the master of the house was what they needed. So back Bosco came. We found a home for him as a Companion Dog, and last I heard he was definitely enjoying life."

"And the man who needed him?"

"He came back for another training session and went home with a dog who took work seriously. They are getting on just fine."

Willa thought of Honey and all she did that was almost taken for granted. "They do work, don't they?"

"Twenty-four hours a day, or whenever a sound alerts them. A Hearing Dog is an ambassador for the program, which reminds me that you may soon be approached by clubs and organizations in the area asking you to demonstrate with Honey and tell about the program."

Willa looked startled and shook her head. "Oh, I couldn't. I can't stand up in front of people and talk. I—I—"

"But you've told me that Honey is making it easier for you to approach people."

"That's one-to-one. I couldn't stand up before a whole roomful. I'd be so nervous I wouldn't have any words."

"Even so, you wouldn't be doing the demonstration. That would be up to Honey."

"Perhaps."

Gently, persuasively, the instructor explained that this was something Willa should be willing to do for the program so that more and more people would know what Hearing Dogs are and what they can do. "The attention will all be on Honey. She won't let you down, and it's up to you not to let the program down."

Willa still felt reluctant, although she had to agree that the reasoning was valid. "I guess I'm the one who has the problem." Then she thought of the zippers. "I do have a question," she said. And she described Honey's interest in removing zippers. "It's the only mischievous thing she's ever done, but why does she have to do it?"

"Perhaps I can give you an answer. You may recall the time in class when your instructor told you all about the backgrounds of the different dogs, where they came from, and how they arrived at the shelters? There wasn't one who had not been through a rugged experience, and Honey's was one of the saddest. Do you remember it?"

Willa shook her head. What she remembered was that she had been so entranced with Honey and their new relationship that she hadn't kept her eyes on the instructor when she was telling the early histories of the dogs. She remembered, too, that she had not wanted to know where Honey came from, just that she was all hers. "I wasn't paying attention and no one told me," she said.

The instructor nodded. "I think this will explain everything. One of our staff was driving along a country road and noticed a bag in a ditch. It seemed to be moving. She got out of her car to investigate. Looking more closely, she saw that it was a canvas bag with a zippered fastening. The fastening had been worked apart at one end and a puppy head was peering out from it. She picked up the bag and tore it open so the puppy could get some air. There were two others in the bottom of the bag, but the one whose little teeth tore the zipper apart was the only one that survived. It was Honey. Our staff took her right to a vet, but it was a day or two before he was sure she would make it."

Honey, hearing her name, pressed close to Willa, whose arms went around her in the warmest embrace she had ever given.

Sympathetically, the instructor watched them for a minute; then she added, "There seems to be no end to the means people will take to rid themselves of unwanted animals when it could be so simple: a trip to the vet and a request for euthanasia. But that often costs money."

Willa had no words. Pride in Honey and thankfulness that she had managed to live filled her heart and mind.

"When a request comes up for a demonstration, you'll need some help," the instructor went on. "It always takes two. Shall I drive over, or do you have someone near who could lend a hand?"

A shy smile that spoke of inner happiness stole over Willa's face. "I think I can get someone to help."

When the outreach worker left, it was with high commendation. "You two are a good match. You have a sound relationship. Honey is doing as much for you as you are for her."

Chapter Seven

By now, Willa was quite accustomed to meeting Rosey with some of her friends. This Saturday morning Rosey brought her teacher to the park and proudly introduced Miss Spencer to "my special friends, Willa and Honey." It was not long before Rosey ran off with Honey to play Frisbee.

With practice they had both become better. Rosey was adept now at hurling the plastic disc. It whirled high with Honey's eyes upon it, her whole body quivering with excitement as she tried to anticipate where it might land. Then she leaped to catch it, doing a whirlabout in the air as she brought it down. She played with it for a moment, even tossed it up on her own, ran off with it, then spun around and raced back to Rosey with it in her mouth.

"Give," Rosey said, and Honey dropped the disc, all eagerness for it to be thrown again.

Miss Spencer and Willa had been having a game of their own. Miss Spencer asked Willa if she would come to the school the following Wednesday afternoon and show the children what a Hearing Dog could do for deaf people.

"They know something about handicaps since we have a legally blind child in the class," said Miss Spencer. "The girl has her Braille books and some special teaching; she keeps up well with the others. They help her in many ways. To have you and Honey for a visit would extend their understanding."

Willa was glad to have people know what Honey could do. Before she had a chance to feel shy about it, she had said yes and set a time for their visit to the school. Mr. Locke had told her more than once that she would be welcome to a few hours off occasionally when there was an opportunity to present Honey and her skills to others. As a sponsor of the program, he felt it was in everyone's interest to know more about the Hearing Dogs.

Breathless and panting from their game, Rosey and Honey returned to hear the news. Impulsively Rosey threw her arms around Willa and gave her a big hug; then she did the same for Honey. "And I'll be your interpreter," she said gleefully, "if you need one."

"The children will ask you questions," Miss Spencer warned, "and they can be very frank in what they want to know."

"I'll try to be ready for them."

When Willa got home, with the rest of the day before her and all the odd tasks that a Saturday presented, she began to have misgivings. What had she gotten herself into! But it was too late to change her mind, and she could not disappoint Rosey.

That Wednesday, Willa presented herself promptly at the school. Rosey and a committee of three had been appointed to greet her and lead her to the fourth-grade classroom. A WELCOME sign had been hung on Miss Spencer's desk, and a bowl of water for Honey had been placed on the floor. It was Rosey's honor to introduce her friends; and as she did, she explained that they would demonstrate a few of the sounds that Honey knew, but they couldn't show all of them.

Miss Spencer gave Willa a timer and asked her to set it for the amount of time she would need for the demonstration. After that, there would be questions. Willa set it for ten minutes. A boy in the front row stood up. "If she is deaf, how will she hear our questions?"

Rosey had her answer ready. "Look right at Miss Macy; speak clearly and not loudly. She will read your lips."

Willa returned the timer to Miss Spencer; and, with Honey close to her left knee, she faced the class and told them that the first step in all training was basic obedience. Honey was cooperative in doing the commands with which she was familiar: *heel, sit, down, come*. Each one was accompanied by a hand signal. Sensing the occasion, she performed in a lively way, sometimes anticipating a command before Willa gave it. No one noticed during the exercises that Miss Spencer had slipped out of the room and closed the door behind her. Willa described a few different sounds and the way Honey alerted her to them; then there was a loud knocking on the door.

Honey ran to the door, back to Willa, then to the door again. Willa, following her, opened the door, and in walked Miss Spencer. The children cheered and clapped their hands. A moment later the timer on the desk went off. Honey faced the sound, nudged Willa's knee, then looked earnestly at her. She raced to the desk, cocked her head at the timer that was still buzzing, and ran back to Willa, who was still standing by the door with Miss Spencer. Honey was ready to run back and forth until Willa got the message, went to the desk, picked up the timer, and turned it off. Then Willa faced the class.

"With these two sounds you can see the way she gets my attention," Willa said. "Actually, she demands my attention." She leaned toward Honey and embraced her. "Thank you, Honey, you're a good girl. Now lie down and rest for a while." Honey would have preferred to keep performing, but Willa used a tone and a gesture that must be obeyed.

Then came the questions.

"Is it harder to be deaf than to be blind?"

Willa lifted her shoulders and held out her hands. "Who can say? Blindness sometimes brings out a sort of kindness from people; deafness tends to make people annoyed. They talk more loudly. That does no good and makes it harder for the lip reader. People can imagine being blind by closing their eyes and keeping them closed. It is not easy for a hearing person to shut out all sound and imagine being deaf. A person who is blind may wear dark glasses or carry a white cane; deafness is invisible. It has no identification except for those who can benefit from a hearing aid."

She leaned over to pick up Honey's leash and held it so all could see the words HEARING DOG. "Now, when people see me with Honey, they know why I have not answered when they call to me; why I smile a little vaguely because I have not been able to understand what they are saying. Honey comes to my rescue and—would you believe it?—people sometimes talk to her and expect her to relay their words to me!"

A girl sitting in the third row said, "I have a good imagination, but I can't imagine what it would be like to be deaf."

A small voice near the rear said, "I can." The little girl was wearing large dark glasses and her fingers were busy with a stylus, making Braille notes.

"What is it like?" someone asked.

"It is like living in a prison of silence, and it can be very lonely," Willa replied. Her tone was gentle, her words matter-of-fact. "I was not always deaf, and so when I see the branches of a tree moving, or stand by a lake where water laps the shore, I can remember what the sounds were like. They make a music in my mind."

"Do you watch TV?"

"Yes, when the words are printed with the picture or when someone off to one side is signing. That is how I learned about Hearing Dogs. I saw them on a TV program."

The children were moved. Their questions went beyond curiosity into awareness of a whole other way of living, and from awareness into a desire to help.

A boy in the back row spoke up. "There are so many things you can do for a person who is blind—read to them, offer help, guide them, cut up their food. What can we do for a person who is deaf?"

Willa's answer came slowly. "You can speak clearly, face the person directly, use your hands and facial expressions to support your words—show them you care."

Rosey was bouncing up and down on her toes. She gave a signal and the class stood. Individually and together they all made the three signs Rosey had taught them, the signs that said "I love you."

The smile that flickered occasionally on Willa's face became steady. "That is the most important thing of all," she said. She put her hand on Honey's head. "Honey shows what love is, what love can do."

An hour later, at home, Willa looked at Honey and laughed. "Do you know what we've just done? We've given a demonstration!"

* * * * *

The alarm was not set to go off on Sunday mornings, but often when Willa awoke she discovered Honey standing by her bed, tail gently waving, eyes looking at her. Honey's anticipation turned to joy when Willa finally pulled herself out of the covers and fumbled for her slippers. One Sunday when Willa closed the window, she had to brush away a slight accumulation of snow that had fallen during the night. Then she stood still, watching the flakes as they drifted slowly down. No need to wonder whether they were making any sound; she remembered from the time she was a little girl that snow was the quietest of nature's offerings; only a wind could make it swish, and there was no wind today.

"Honey, see what's waiting for you!" she exclaimed, going to the kitchen door and opening it.

For a moment Honey stood poised in surprise, then she ran into the snow, pushed her nose along and through it, rolled and shook free, rolled again, then leaped and did one of her air somersaults. She was having such fun that she seemed to have forgotten the purpose of her being let out. Willa watched her, sharing the abandonment, remembering. When Willa finally called Honey in, she came readily enough, eager for her breakfast. Willa rubbed her with a towel, then she dried one paw after another, checking between the pads for snow. Honey relished the attention and lapped at Willa's face with her long tongue.

Two letters were propped up on the kitchen table. They had come earlier in the week and Willa had saved them to answer on Sunday: one was from a service club, the other from a women's group in a neighboring town. Had they come a month ago, fearfulness would have given her the only answer: "No, sorry." Since her afternoon at the school, her only answer could be "Yes, gladly." She looked down at Honey. "It will be your show."

Honey heard the knocking at the front door and went back and forth from it to Willa until she convinced Willa that it was not because she wanted to go out again in the snow but because someone wanted to come in. It was Denis, snow shovel in hand, and behind him Willa could see that the front walk was cleared and clean. She asked him to come in, and Honey danced around him until he was sitting at the kitchen table. He drank coffee and listened to Willa telling him about the two letters, asking him to read them. His response was what she had secretly hoped for, but it took her by surprise when it came so soon.

"I'll help too—I can drive you there," he offered. "Then I'll be handy for anything."

"Will you let me help you with the bundles of clothing tomorrow evening?" Willa asked.

"Indeed yes, and Honey too."

He refused a second cup of coffee, his eyes on the clock. "The Sunday service is at eleven. Coming with me? Honey may be the first dog ever inside St. Martin's, but if your work goes the way it's going, she won't be the last."

When Honey saw her leash come down from its hook and felt Willa attaching it to her collar, she thumped her tail on the floor and licked Willa's hand in anticipation.

Chapter Eight

For a long time, life had been like a straight road for Willa, one mile the same as the other, and she had no reason to think it would ever be different. She had learned to live within her restrictions, and if there was something called joy, she found it in muted ways. Now life had become a road with views and vistas and turnings; no mile was like the one she had already traveled.

That Sunday afternoon, she replied to the two letters, agreeing to the arrangements already suggested and saying that she would come with a friend who would help with some of the details. After daily practice with Honey and one trial run with Denis, she felt ready for the first of the two successive Friday evenings. The meeting was in a hall large enough for chairs to be spaced comfortably, with an open area at the front where Willa would work. Honey was taken off her leash and began to wander at will among the audience. Willa nodded assent, knowing it was the only way Honey's responses could be natural and spontaneous.

The chairman made a brief introduction, then he spoke from the notes Willa had given him about the NEADS program. "Miss Macy has requested that no matter how appealing Honey is, when she goes up to you, please do not give her any kind of tidbit. That may come later when we have refreshments. There are six basic sounds that every Hearing Dog is trained to respond to. Some people have special requirements and their dogs will be trained to them." He turned to Willa. "How many sounds does Honey have now?"

Willa lifted six fingers. Honey was learning more, but she did not want to put her through them tonight.

The chairman sat down and Willa went to the table where an alarm clock was clearly visible. She set it to go off in two minutes; then she stretched out on the couch that was near and closed her eyes as if in sleep. Honey was wandering around the room, greeting people with a lap of her tongue or a wag of her tail.

The alarm went off. Honey lifted her head, stood still for a moment, then raced past the people in the chairs. She ran across the open space to stand beside the couch and push her nose against Willa's cheek. She nuzzled Willa until Willa got off the couch and embraced her. Everyone in the room heard Willa saying, "Good girl! Such a good girl." On a nearby stand was a telephone. It began to ring loudly and persistently. Honey was not familiar with telephones, but she knew that any bell must be attended to; so she directed Willa to the phone.

The attention of the audience shifted to a door at the far end of the hall. Someone most certainly wanted to get in, since the knocking could be heard by all, especially Honey, who ran to the door then back to Willa. Together they went to the door. Willa opened it, and Honey's ecstasy was unbounded when she saw who it was: Denis.

Then the smoke alarm screeched. It startled everyone and its insistency made some people nervous. Honey was the calmest in the room. She went to the sound, then to the nearest outside exit and there she waited. Willa realized what Honey's moves meant and crossed the room to go to her. Putting her hand on the door, she opened it and both went out. When the smoke alarm was silenced, they returned to the room.

From the small kitchen where refreshments were being prepared, a tea kettle started to whistle. Honey went to Willa, who made no move; then she went to the kitchen and returned to Willa.

"She wants her to do something about it," a woman in the audience whispered loudly.

And Willa did. She followed Honey into the kitchen and turned the stove off.

"If there's nothing more, we will now adjourn for refreshments," the chairman said. Then he turned to thank Willa and to commend Honey. But there was something more.

From a seat in the back row, a baby started to cry. Honey, standing close beside Willa, looked up at her questioningly. Willa saw a young woman trying to quiet her little one. She saw the small mouth opening wide, the tears sliding down the cheeks. Honey knew what to do. She ran to the sound, then back to Willa. Her whole being, including the moving tail, was a question mark. Willa put her hand on the golden head. "Go," she said, shaping the word carefully. "Do what you can."

And Honey did, returning to lap the baby's wet cheeks until a smile shone through the tears.

"She's never practiced that sound with me," Willa said to no one in particular.

And yet, perhaps she had.

A man in the front row stood up with an envelope in his hands. "We want to do something for the program. Would Honey help us here?"

Willa took Honey's head between her palms, then pointed to the man. Honey trotted over to him and took the envelope in her glove-soft lips. It was not even moist when she presented it to Willa. This was a first for Honey, and she handled it with grace and dignity. Willa thought of the stories she had heard of how little Molly would race around a room and collect dollar bills, then race back to the instructor or trainer.

The demonstration was over. Willa begged to be excused from the refreshments, and Denis agreed, knowing that it would be too difficult for Willa to converse with people whose lips might be involved with eating. Honey was reluctant to leave, but after a signal from Willa and a slight tug on the leash, she submitted. She knew she had done what she was supposed to do. Her reward came from the admiration she received and the hands reaching out to stroke her as she left the hall and went toward the car.

Together Denis drove them to a small restaurant that looked attractive as well as expensive. At the door they were met by a pleasant but firm host. "Sorry, but we do not allow dogs with our patrons. Please leave the animal in your car."

"This is a specially trained dog," Denis said.

Willa held out her ID card with Honey's name and picture and the words of explanation that Hearing Dogs must now be legally accepted in all public places. There was nothing for the host to do but admit them with a smile that was barely a smile. Honey kept close to Willa and tucked herself neatly under the table between the two pairs of friendly legs.

"You're tired," said Denis. It was not a question; it was a statement of fact.

Willa found it easy to reply. "Yes, I always am after I project my voice for any length of time, but I was proud of Honey. She really did it all."

"Not quite all; you touched them too, Willa."

"Talk to me, Denis. I'd always rather listen than talk."

"Even when listening demands concentration on your part?"

"Even then."

An hour later when they left, the host went to the door with them. "Your dog has behaved better than many of our patrons. Will you present this to her when you get home, with our compliments?''

In the bag handed to her, Willa felt the shape of a marrow bone.

* * * * *

Early in the year, Willa received an envelope bearing the return address of the Hearing Dog training center she had attended. Inside was a letter that went out to all the graduates of the program.

NEW ENGLAND ASSISTANCE DOG SERVICE

Hi! Happy New Year to you from all of us at NEADS. Here is our annual survey that we use to follow up on your progress with your dog and to find out if there are any problems that we can help you solve. We would appreciate it if you could take time to answer the following questions. Your reply will help us evaluate our training program. Please complete and return the questionnaire by February 20. Thank you.

Pencil in hand, Willa took pleasure in answering the various questions, filling in first her name and then Honey's.

1. *Is your dog responding to all the sounds that it was trained to do?*
2. *Have you taught your dog to respond to any new sounds?*
3. *Do you find that you have the time to practice every day? If not, how often do you practice?*
4. *How is your dog's basic obedience?*
5. *Do you take your dog to stores and restaurants?*
6. *Any other general comments?*

Willa felt that one big *yes* could answer all the questions. She was glad now that she had been asked to do the demonstrations, for they gave her examples for the "general comments." What could she say except to describe how well Honey had done—almost too well—for she clearly liked to show off, and the attention she received was her delight. Willa thought of a question of her own: What would happen to the world if we all acted out of love and were satisfied with love as our reward?

Carefully, she refolded the questionnaire and sealed it in an envelope. At least this was one letter she was happy to answer and return long before the required date.

Chapter Nine

It was a mild evening, with the first warm hint of spring in the air. The windows were open, and there was fragrance. Denis and Willa had been having supper together on Friday nights for several weeks, often at Willa's, occasionally going out to a restaurant. Their conversations filled blanks about each other's lives. Willa knew about Denis's parents, that they had died some time ago and that Mr. Locke had done much as a substitute parent. Conscious of what Honey was doing for her, Willa longed to know what Pundit had done for Denis.

"Why did you call him Pundit?" she asked on that particular evening. "Doesn't it mean some kind of a teacher?"

Denis nodded. "He came with the name as a four-month-old pup, but he grew into it. He was a teacher by nature—perhaps all dogs are. We did everything together, and he made himself as pleasing to my mother as to my father; so he was with me wherever I went. We were necessary to each other. I didn't matter much to my parents, except as a minor tax deduction, but I did matter to Pundit. In my early teens our gang started doing some foolish things, not always bad, but they could have had consequences. And they did. There was one—'' he turned away.

"Don't get off the track," Willa said, "keep on with the story."

Facing her again, he smiled an apology and went on. "When I'd get home from one of our escapades, Pundit would look at me with eyes that almost looked through me. They seemed so calm and wise, not exactly reproachful, but wondering. He went to college with me, and they let me keep him in the dorm. By the time I graduated he was beginning to show his years. I resented that, because the years at college were fitting me for living. That was when I began to let him teach me, since I saw through him what time did to life."

For a minute Denis paused, thinking back. Then he went on. "I resisted, he accepted. Tranquillity for Pundit was a warm place in the sun or a cool place in the shade. He kept his head up and his gaze was always forward, as if he saw things that I couldn't see. Then, one day last summer . . .'' Denis turned away but he continued talking.

Willa leaned toward him and put her hands gently on his cheeks, turning his face back to her. "I want to have it all. We've shared the richness; now we must share the other. It will be the same for me someday, and Honey."

With words coming inevitably like sand through an hourglass, Denis told her of the day that he knew had to be his last with Pundit. "He was a great age by then, sixteen. His sight had dimmed, and his hearing. In rain or snow he easily became disoriented, and he did not move with freedom. He had given me a reason to live; and I, because it was the one last gift I had for him, gave him the means to die. The vet told me what to do. My heart was aching, but something in me was soaring—a life lived nobly could die nobly, and by the hand of the one who had been loved and served."

Denis came to the end of his story, realizing that Willa's eyes had not left his face. "I've never said this before. No one has ever listened to me the way you do."

"It's what I can do."

"I've needed someone to listen to me."

"I've needed someone to talk to me."

Denis put his head in his hands. Willa sat back in her chair, aware of something so blessed that there were no words for it. They had shared much during the past months, as they grew to know each other; now they were sharing sorrow. She did not want to reach out and touch his hands, or do what she had not yet done, embrace him. It would look as if she was offering comfort or pity, and those he did not need.

Honey had been sitting near the window of the house where the scents and sounds of the warm evening flowed. There had been no reason for her to be alert, but she had not been asleep. Scarcely making a sound, she crossed the room to stand beside Denis's chair; then with sure motions she lapped his face, slowly, softly, giving her affection in the way she had to give it and asking nothing in return.

Some time later, when Denis said good-bye in the doorway, his arms went around Willa. Her arms found their way. Their lips met. He could not speak; she would not have heard.

* * * * *

The first Monday evening of the month had become part of the pattern of living. Willa and Honey, returning from work, had a brief play time in the back yard and an early supper. Then Willa changed her clothes and along with Honey met Denis on the porch at St. Martin's. The days were longer now and their work could be done outside in the daylight; the piles of clothes were getting bigger, as if people were cleaning out their too-used clothes or not-enough-used winter clothes to get ready for another season.

''The usual,'' Denis commented as he gestured to the accumulation on the lawn: some were bundles of neatly folded clean clothes, others scarcely worth looking at.

Invariably Denis found something for Honey, and this time he held up a pair of cut-off shorts, paint-stained and torn, but with a splendid zipper. He tossed it to Honey, who raced off with it. She soon left the shorts and went to a pile of rejects in a corner and began rooting around in it. She stood still for a moment, cocked her head, then went to Willa and nudged her. Willa gave her a pat, used to Honey's moments when all she seemed to want was recognition, but this was different. Honey went back to the pile, nosed it, then returned to Willa.

Denis said, "Why is she barking?"

"I can see she is: that means attention."

Denis looked at the pile. "Sounds as if a cricket was down in there. We'll get to it in a few minutes."

"Is May the month for crickets?" Willa asked. "Honey is telling me something. I can't put her off any longer." Willa left the sorting she was doing and went to the pile of miscellaneous oddments. Honey watched her, wagging her tail, pleased as she always was when she got her message through.

Willa's hands fumbled in the pile. "Why, it's an alarm clock, with a knobby sock attached to it, and it's still ticking! Good girl."

Suddenly Denis was by her side. Seizing the clock and the sock that looked as if it had been stuffed with an assortment of oddly shaped balls, he threw it as far as he could across the lawn. He laid a restraining hand on Honey so she wouldn't chase it, saying "It's not a clock; it's a little bomb." He turned to face Willa and repeated his words. "It didn't get in with the clothes; it was put in. Did you see what time the alarm was set for?"

Willa had. "Eight-thirty."

The church clock above them had only recently struck eight. "Then we've time to put it out of commission. Keep Honey while I get some water to dowse it with; then I'll bury it."

Willa sat down on the porch steps and held Honey close to her as she watched Denis approach the innocent looking clock with its stuffed sock tail. He poured two pails of water on it, used his knife to detach the clock, then dug a hole for the rest and stamped the earth down over it. When he came back, he sat beside Willa and gave Honey the praise she enjoyed.

"You just thought it was a new kind of Frisbee—good girl." He turned full-face to Willa. "It was a very little bomb; so it couldn't have done much harm, perhaps started a small fire just after we had left—if it hadn't been discovered."

"But why? But who?"

Denis held out his hands, palms up, a gesture well known between them that took the place of words. "A prank, but sometimes a prank can have consequences." He rolled the clock over and studied it. "I think I know who did this. I'll try to have a talk with him."

"But why? Something against the church?"

"Not the church—against life, the world, and he thinks he can make a protest this way. I could have done something like this once."

"And that's why you want to work—to keep youngsters from doing things like this?"

"Much more. To divert their energies into constructive channels. What seems a prank—and that's all this alarm clock is—can have serious consequences."

"Consequences." Willa repeated the last word. "Like what?"

Denis was silent, shaking his head slowly as he sat down on the steps of the church.

Willa joined him there and reminded him of her question. "Like what?"

At first, as he described some of the escapades he and his gang had engaged in, he faced her, but more often he looked ahead of himself and Willa missed his words. She did not care. Once she laid her hand on his knee and said, "It's you now, Denis, that I know. I don't need to be told about the things you did; they are far behind you."

He shook his head. "I want you to know." His lips, usually so mobile, were tightly set and even when he faced her she did not get his words clearly; but this seemed to be something he needed to say, and the word *consequences* kept coming through to her.

In the silences between them and in her loss of some of his words, Willa went back to something she had put out of her mind but could never forget—the time when a firecracker had been tied to her pigtail. Consequences. No one ever found out who did it, but had she wanted to she could have told Denis that she knew something about consequences. The person who did it most likely did not know her, had nothing against her; it was a prank—it would make a big noise. Those who had been nearby reported that a group of hoodlums had run off laughing; they had disappeared into the crowd that had gathered for a Fourth of July celebration.

In a gesture that she had not used for years, Willa put her hand up to the back of her head the way she used to when she wore a pigtail.

Denis did not see her; his head was in his hands and the last word she was aware of him saying was *regret*.

"But it's regret that has made you want to do something with your life," she said softly.

He nodded.

"Then perhaps it was worth it."

Then Willa stared ahead of her, lost in her own remembering. She did not see the tears that traveled slowly down Denis's cheeks revealing what a tortuous journey he had made back into the misdeeds of his past. There was nothing Willa could do, but Honey knew what was needed. She licked Denis's face and made whimpering sounds. He put his arm around her and drew her close. Willa's arm had been circling Honey, and their hands met, then their eyes.

"I've been trying to tell you these things about me for a long time."

"And I wouldn't listen. It doesn't matter, Denis; it's what you are now, what you have ahead of you to do."

"With your help."

The clock in the tower above them struck the half hour. The hands of the alarm clock were in agreement, and Willa suddenly remembered the homemade bomb that Denis had buried. But neither sound nor movement came from the small fresh mound on the side of the lawn. Darkness was coming down; so Denis put the pails and shovel away. Willa straightened the tumbled pile that had held the clock while Honey waited patiently. It was one of the times when she was not needed; so she sat still, ready for the signal to move whenever it should come.

* * * * *

It seemed to Willa that there was something inevitable about the relationship between her and Denis. It had existed from the day when Honey's brief excursion into the big world had brought him into their lives. After their first hesitancy, Willa and Denis had begun to enjoy discovering each other. They had helped each other. They had shared deep thoughts. Willa could agree with Mr. Locke that Denis Talcot was indeed "a nice young fellow," but now he was becoming so much more.

As the weeks and months went on and winter yielded to spring and spring to the future, part of the inevitability was that they should make plans.

"I will have the degree I'm working for in June," Denis told her.

"And then?"

"Then I want to have an office of my own and be available to young people who need to talk; who need someone to listen."

"How will you find them?"

"I'll go to schools and visit with teachers. There are many young people to whom I'll make the approach myself."

Willa fell silent, remembering her own troubled teen-age years, wondering what it would have meant if there had been someone with whom she could talk. Denis would make a difference in many young lives. And she would be glad when it was June. "June," she repeated aloud, saying it slowly. The thought brought forth the feeling of warm days, the sight of flowers and their growing, the smell of mown grass. There would be birds, and she could hear their songs inwardly when she watched the vibrations of their throats.

Again there was a silence.

"I've asked for my two weeks of vacation the last part of June," Willa remarked. "That's when the Dog Show is being held. It will be a reunion for Honey's class, but there will be other dogs there from other classes too."

"I'd like to drive you and Honey there." Speaking of June and the weekend plans gave Denis the opportunity to mention his hopes of other plans that would involve them both.

Willa was still hesitant of anything that brought her too much before people. "Not a big church," she said, so softly that Denis barely caught the words.

"The town clerk has more than dog licenses."

Willa smiled with relief, then she beamed. "Something quiet and plain." She slipped her hand into his.

"But no less real and binding."

"Shall we say *bonding?* I've learned to love that word."

Chapter Ten

Willa had the better part of a week to think of what was impending in her life, for Denis would be away until Saturday. With only Honey to confide in, she began to have misgivings. Was it being fair, she asked herself, to burden Denis Talcot with her problem, to impose her deafness on so young a man whose life was before him, whose career was in his hands?

He wanted to learn to sign and she would teach him, but it was difficult and it took a long time before one became adept. Willa compelled herself to think of all they could not share, like listening to music or watching a play, unless it was miming. And her own voice, which she did not hear, modulated by the implant she wore in one ear—wouldn't he grow tired in time of that one tone? It devastated her to think of these things, but she felt she must face them and find her own answers.

"Honey, Honey, what should I do?" she exclaimed.

She could withdraw, see him once more, and then never again. He would disagree, but in the end it might be better to hurt him now than have a hurt go through his whole life.

Honey often sensed when Willa was deep in troubling thoughts. Now, as she had done before, she placed herself in front of Willa and their eyes held each other. Willa talked on in a murmuring way. Honey listened, and eventually drew her tongue across the back of Willa's hand.

"You're right, Honey; we've gone far enough and I'm getting nowhere. Let's go for a walk in the park."

Willa hoped to see Rosey, and she did, but it was a different Rosey who came running across the grass. The little girl had eyes for no one but Honey.

"I need you, Honey," she said as she dropped down beside the dog and wrapped her arms about her.

Willa did not hear the words, but the attitude told her enough. She went to the bench where they had so often sat to talk and read and sign together, knowing that when Rosey had shared her secret or sorrow or shame or whatever it was with Honey, she would join her.

And she did.

"I needed to talk to someone who wouldn't talk back to me," Rosey announced as she sat down beside Willa and pushed her hair back from her face.

The story came out in breathless haste. Although Willa did not get it all, since Rosey often forgot to look at her but addressed herself to Honey or to the wide open air, she understood enough to know that it was a minor tragedy. Rosey had broken a china horse belonging to her best friend.

"And she thought I did it on purpose—" Rosie gasped, trying to say how it happened. "And she kept talking back so fast that I couldn't explain—" she struggled with a sob. "And I needed someone who wouldn't talk back and there was Honey." She threw her arms around Willa. "You'll listen, won't you, and let me tell how it happened?"

"I'll listen," Willa said. In a flash of time, the scene changed and she saw herself saying those very words to Denis when he came home in the evening needing to have someone listen to him. She returned Rosey's embrace. "We all need each other, Rosey, and perhaps we should be able to say that more often than we do."

They talked about other things; they did some signing; and, for lack of a Frisbee, Rosey threw sticks for Honey, who raced gleefully in pursuit and retrieval. When it was time to leave, Willa took Rosey's hands in hers and looked at her in the same way that she looked at Honey, eyes searching eyes. "Just say two very simple words when you see your friend Patsy again: 'I'm sorry.' She'll listen."

"Do you really think so?"

"I really do."

Willa had Saturday chores to do, but the one that lightened the day was preparing supper. Denis would be back in town by six o'clock with news of his final exams and more plans for the future. He would look at her in a way that said as clearly as any words "All is well, isn't it?" And she would reply, "All is well."

She could not account to herself how it was that her misgivings had vanished. All she knew was that a simple equation had been worked out: she needed him and he needed her. In admitting something that had grown between them almost without their knowing it, they would acknowledge a debt that each owed the other.

* * * * *

A few weeks later in the town clerk's office, with Honey beside them, they raised their right hands and made their promises. As with so much that had happened during the past months, it was as simple as that.

Once at home, Willa was eager to have Denis see the new word she had been teaching Honey. "I'm going to our room, and I'll close the door, or almost close it. It's an arrangement Honey and I have had for a long time. She knows I don't need her for awhile, and she amuses herself. After a few minutes, call her to you, take her head in your hands, look at her earnestly, and ask her to find *Mrs. Talcot.*"

Willa left and went to the other room, partly closing the door. Denis let several minutes go by; then he called Honey, looked into her eyes, and said, "Go, find Mrs. Talcot."

Honey seemed uncertain. She turned her head one way, then another, only to see that there was no familiar person in the room with them. She looked back at Denis, searching his face. He repeated the words.

Suddenly, with a flash of motion and a tail wagging hard enough to propel her body, she swung around and ran to the half-open door. She pushed it with her nose, saw Willa, and hurled herself against her.

"Thank you, Honey, that's a good girl!" Willa's praise was lavish. "Now, go back to Denis."

Honey whirled around and ran to throw herself against him.

* * * * *

Denis did not need Willa's careful directions about the various turns in the road as they approached the place where the dog show was being held. He could already hear the dogs, for a medley of barks filled the air. Rounding the last turn, they drove into a parking space. Willa attached the leash to Honey's collar, to remind the dog that from this moment on she would be working. Denis saw the chairs on the lawn where onlookers were gathering, and he found a place among them. Willa and Honey went off to join the score or more of dogs that were all bonded to their owners, all proclaiming what they were by their orange collars and leashes.

People were talking together, renewing friendships: those who were speech readers, silently; those who were signers, gesturing; those who could benefit by hearing aids, audibly. The instructor and the trainers moved among them all, talking and signing. Willa had caught the instructor's eye as she and Denis came across the lawn, and the warmth of the smile that embraced them gave her an assurance that went beyond words. There was no time for talk, although there would be later. Right now everyone was paying attention to the dogs.

"How's Emily?"

"Fantastic! I fractured my leg last fall and had it in a cast, but she adjusted her pace to mine. Once I tripped and lost my cane, but Emily picked it up and gave it to me. At night she carries my flashlight.''

"And Cookie?"

"There never was such a dog! She even heard a mouse nibbling in the cupboard and told me to do something about it.''

"Laddie?"

"Not always good on the alarm clock, because he knows once he wakes me I'll soon be leaving him. He still has a lot to learn about names—he confuses Debbie with Daddy.''

"Jack?"

"He's a miracle dog, does everything and much more, but he does oversleep once or twice a week.''

"And Ebony?"

"She took second in an Obedience Class and is on her way with points toward a C.D.—Companion Dog.''

"And Honey?"

"She saved my life from loneliness." There was so much more for Willa to say, but it was time to move on to the events.

"We told you it was a working partnership and a growing process. I'm proud of you all," the instructor said. "Now, into the ring and line up with the dogs from other classes. There are prizes for all the firsts.''

Denis, sitting on the lawn that sloped down to the ring, was in the midst of similar conversation as friends and families talked about what the dogs had done in their homes.

"Nugget's unselfish love gave Joan back her life."

"Our boy couldn't seem to make friends in school, but Captain made them for him, and now he's tops in everything."

"Our house would have burned down if Kelpie hadn't discovered that the stove was on and awakened my wife. The neighbors heard the barking, but it took more than barking, and Kelpie knew it."

"It's love in action; that's all you can say about these dogs."

The parade formed in the ring. Dogs and their owners walked slowly around so the audience could see the participants and the judges could begin their determinations. Denis, reading the program, felt sure that Honey would win every class.

Best Groomed came first; and though Honey's coat shone and the feathery hair on her legs had been trimmed, the prize went to another dog. Then came *Basic Obedience.* Honey did all she was asked to do, but she was slow on the *down* command because she was too interested in all that was going on around her. She did not even place for a first in *Special Tricks* since Jack outran, outleaped, and outsomersaulted her in Frisbee catching. She did not shine as *Superdog,* a test to demonstrate steadiness and control in different situations. She held back at one of the obstacles and stood in front of Willa, blocking her way; not sure herself, she would not impose something unknown on her owner.

The last class was for *Best Tail Wag,* and the program indicated that dogs would be judged on technique, rhythm, and style. Honey's tail never stopped wagging; it went up and down and crosswise, and even turned like a clock hand. The award went to a small dog whose tail never lost momentum but was always in perfect rhythm.

There was one award left. It marked the culmination of all the classes and had been kept in mind throughout the competition by judges and trainers as they determined which dog had improved most during the year since training. Again the participants lined up, dogs at heel, handlers standing quietly, occasionally reaching down to stroke a head or murmur an encouraging word.

The instructor stepped forward to make the announcement, signing and speaking. "This is, perhaps, the most important of the awards since it shows what has been happening between one person and one dog during the past year. There is no question in the minds of the judges and trainers: the one showing the most improvement is Honey."

Honey heard her name before Willa caught its significance, and she stepped forward, drawing Willa with her.

"And Willa, of course," the instructor said as she presented the trophy to the surprised and delighted Willa.

Speaking to everyone present as well as to Willa, the instructor continued, "We were not entirely sure how it would work out last summer. We knew Honey needed someone to whom she could be everything, and that is not always possible in every household. Only by being totally responsible would Honey be able to show the confidence that's needed in a Hearing Dog.''

Willa's smile, often so fleeting, did not fade. ''But it is Honey who has given me confidence.''

''Then you both deserve the award, and it proves that our decision was right.''

The participants clapped, the onlookers clapped, and the dogs barked. Willa and Honey, walking proudly together with their trophy, went to join Denis.

They watched as recognition was given to many different people and organizations who were making the program possible by their sponsorship. Then they enjoyed a picnic with the kind of food that owners could share with their dogs. It ended with much talk and laughter, with assurances made to each other that they would meet again at the next dog show, and then it was time for good-byes.

When at last Willa and Denis went to the car, Honey crawled in and flattened out on the back seat. She was tired, and she didn't care who knew it. It had been a big day for her, and there was no longer any need to be on duty. She opened one eye, saw that Denis was in the driver's seat, and closed it again. She did not have to help him drive.

The instructor, watching them drive off, turned to the two trainers standing beside her and smiled.

One of the trainers said, ''That was a good match.''

''Yes,'' the other said. ''That *is* a good match.''

A Service Dog can help a young man pursue his dreams—in style. (Michael and Flirt)

Chico, a very special companion, gets the best seat on every trip. (Jean Cohen and Chico)

There's just nothing like a Hearing Dog for a friend and playmate. (Bram Davis and Bagel)

Pick it up? Easy, with a highly trained Service Dog
at your side. (Norman Mooney and J.T.)

A working partnership with his Hearing Dog
makes all the difference in the world to
this dairy farmer. (Robert Barwick and Rerun)